Cover illustration: The Yellow Kid and Uncle Sam Brownie by Mark Wheatley after Palmer Cox and Richard F. Outcault.

POP CULTURE WITH CHARACTER: A LOOK INSIDE GEPPI'S ENTERTAINMENT MUSEUM is a production of Geppi's Entertainment Museum published by Gemstone Publishing Inc. Distributed by Gemstone Publishing Inc.

Geppi's Entertainment Museum
301 W. Camden St.
Baltimore, MD 21201
www.geppismuseum.com

Gemstone Publishing Inc.
1966 Greenspring Dr.
Timonium, MD 21093
www.gemstonepub.com

ISBN-13: 978-1-888472-68-4
ISBN-10: 1-888472-68-5

Printed in the United States of America

10 9 8 7 6 5 4 3 2 1

First Printing: September 2006

A SPECIAL WELCOME
BY STEPHEN A. GEPPI, CEO & OWNER

Geppi's Entertainment Museum (or "GEM," as we call it) is the fulfillment of a lifelong dream to see pop culture entertainment in the setting it deserves. Over the years I have been fortunate enough to be in a position to preserve, promote and present historical comic character collectibles in a variety of venues to the point at which this museum is the next logical step. Take a look around the museum or through the pages of this book and you'll see that the history of popular culture is so tightly woven into the social fabric of the United States of America that it parallels and reinforces mainstream history.

From my earliest days in the comic book business – when I was a child, counting comics for a local store – I have always enjoyed sharing my excitement about the characters with other people. From my brother and the rest of my family, to my friends growing up in Baltimore's Little Italy, to the high profile acquaintances I have made in the business world, spreading the word has been a mission I've taken seriously.

GEM is the next logical step in that mission. It is a showplace of ideas, a marketplace of thought and imagination. In its historic Camden Station setting, it simultaneously looks back across the 230 years of our nation's history and toward the future, offering those who are interested that most significant of all keys to wisdom: understanding.

Our facility is dedicated to the proposition that comic characters – whether entirely fictional or based on figures from real life – have played a hugely successful role in the entertainment and education of children, and in turn that this has played a huge factor in their lives.

It's the spirited, inventive and adventurous kind of learning that captures your mind as a child and stays with you through the rest of your life. This is the same type of education we're promoting through an initiative in Maryland designed to get comics in the hands of school children. Through several of my other companies, we have been involved in a pilot program conceived with Maryland's superb administrators and educators. So, in addition to its other functions, GEM is dedicated to reaching out to those interested in showing the teaching power of the great characters you'll meet in this book.

Whether you've already been through GEM or you're seeing it for the first time in these pages, I hope you will enjoy this book, explore the history it represents, and let your own imagination run wild.

Stephen A. Geppi

After starting Geppi's Comic World in 1974, Steve Geppi launched Diamond Comic Distributors, the largest distributor of English language comic books in the world. In subsequent years he founded Gemstone Publishing, Diamond International Galleries and Diamond Select Toys and acquired other fine firms such as Alliance Game Distributors, Baltimore Magazine, E. Gerber Products, Geppi's Memorabilia Road Show, Hake's Americana & Collectibles, and Morphy Auctions. He is a minority owner of the Baltimore Orioles and is involved in many local civic activities.

Acknowledgements

Geppi's Entertainment Museum
Stephen A. Geppi, Chief Executive Officer and Owner
John K. Snyder, Jr., President
Wendy Kelman, Executive Director
Dr. Arnold T. Blumberg, Curator
Kathie Boozer, Senior Sales Consultant
Andrew Hershberger, Registrar
Julie Meddows, Associate Director of Sales
Jeff Robison, Director of Administration

Gemstone Publishing
Robert M. Overstreet, Publisher/Maryland Office
J.C. Vaughn, Executive Editor/Associate Publisher
Leonard (John) Clark, Editor-in-Chief/Disney Comics
Melissa Bowersox, Director – Creative Projects
Stacia Brown, Editorial Coordinator
Brenda Busick, Creative Director
Russ Cochran, Publisher/Missouri Office
Jamie David, Director of Marketing
Brandon G. DeStefano, Editor
Judy Goodwin, Customer Service Manager
Tom Gordon III, Managing Editor
David Gerstein, Archival Editor/Disney Comics
Mark Huesman, Production Coordinator
Sue Kolberg, Assistant Editor/Disney Comics
Angela Meyer, Traffic and Operations Manager
Sara Ortt, Marketing Assistant
Travis Seitler, Art Director/Disney Comics
Mike Wilbur, Shipping Manager
Heather Winter, Office Manager

Diamond International Galleries
Joshua Geppi, Joe McGuckin, Mark Squirek

**Diamond International Galleries –
   Morphy Auctions**
Dan Morphy, Tom Sage Jr., Katherine Harrigan, Michael
Landis, Kris Lee, Lewis Martin, Zachary Moran, John
C. Morphy, M.D., John K. Morphy, Karen Novak, Erin
Pohronezny, Laura Sciarrino, Natalie Stanilla, Shanelle
Weaver, Leah Witmer, Tema Zerbe.

**Diamond International Galleries –
   Hake's Americana & Collectibles**
Ted Hake, Alex Winter, Michael Bollinger, Joan Carbaugh,
Jack Dixey, Jonell Hake, Mark Herr, Kelly McClain, Kevin
McCray, Linda Snyder, Sarah Snyder, Deak Stagemyer,
Sally Weaver.

Text edited by Dr. Arnold T. Blumberg.

Contributors: David J. Anderson, D.D.S., Dr. Arnold T.
Blumberg, Jaime Bramble, Stacia Brown, Gordon Campbell,
Russ Cochran, Brandon G. DeStefano, David Gerstein,
Gordon Gold, Sam Gold, Tom Gordon III, Ted Hake, Bruce
Hamilton, Katherine Harrigan, Andrew Hershberger, Steve
Ison, Jerry Robinson, Robert M. Overstreet, John K. Snyder,
Jr., J.C. Vaughn, Jerry Weist, Mike Wilbur, Alex Winter.

Cover by Mark Wheatley.

Photography: Mark Huesman, Kelly McClain, Joe
McGuckin, Shanelle Weaver.

Image Processing: Brandon G. DeStefano, Mark Huesman,
Kris Lee, Joe McGuckin, Linda Snyder.

Additional scans courtesy of CGC. Thanks to Mark Salzberg,
Steve Eichenbaum, Steve Borock, Mark Haspel, Paul
Litch, West Stephan, Harshen Patel, Gemma Adel, Scott
Talmadge, and the staff of CGC.

All items pictured in this book, unless otherwise noted, are
from the collection of Stephen A. Geppi.

We gratefully acknowledge all of our lenders, including
those who completed their arrangements after this book
went to press and are therefore not named here: Dr. Arnold
T. Blumberg, Bob Brady, Richard T. Claus, Eric Gewirz, Paul
Hamilton, Russ Harrington, Sheila Harrington, Steve Ison,
Jim Konnerth, Judy Konnerth, Connie Lowe, Jay Lowe,
Steve Meyer, Peter Merolo, Dan Morphy, John C. Morphy,
M.D., Michael Nemeth, Brian Ott, Robert Rogovin, Lori
Sage, Tom Sage, Sr., Michael Solof, Deak Stagemyer, Billy
Tucci, J.C. Vaughn, Alex Winter.

Thanks to Mark Ward and Associates: Mark Ward, Michael
Bouyougas, Miranda Bushey, Jordan Casey, Paul Daniels,
Sam Gallant, Dylan Hay, Catherine Hilsee, Sean Honey,
Bob Jones, Brianna Jones, Alex Lynn, Jeff McGrath, Harry
McMann, Doug Retzler, James Seal, Kim Smutes, Walter
Suitin, James Wade, Amanda Ward, Cecelia Ward; Accent
Display: George Geary; Brite Ideas: Trent Gates, Mark Kooi;
Ely Inc.: Bruce Lee, Abby Krause, Kirk Hoffman, Jorge
Herrera, Erika Johnson; James L. Pierce Custom Framing

Framing by Andrew Shelton (410) 935-1985 and
Sandra Jones (410) 206-9468

Thanks to Explus Inc. - Mike Reyburn, Luis Santana - for
the exquisite case work, 44145 Mercure Circle, Dulles, VA
21066 (703) 260-0780

Thanks to AlphaGraphics, American Visionary Art Museum,
Babe Ruth Birthplace and Museum, The Baltimore
Comic-Con, Cho Benn Holback + Associates, Inc., DC
Comics, Charlie Degliomini, DLA Piper Rudnick Gray Cary
US, LLP, Diamond Comic Distributors, Diamond Select
Toys, Explus Inc., Lipshultz and Hone Chartered, Maryland
Stadium Authority, Reginald F. Lewis Museum of Maryland
African American History & Culture, Catherine Saunders-
Watson, Sports Legends at Camden Yards.

Additional thanks to Benjamin Adams, Adam Anderson,
Robert L. Beerbohm, Marvin & Rochelle Blumberg, Andrew
Bonami, Randy Bowen, Eric C. Caren, Ken Chapman, Kerby
Confer, Stephanie Crawford, Sol M. Davidson, Jeff Dillon,
Anne Ditmeyer, Alan Flenard, Brad Foster, Jim Halperin,
Mark Haynes, Tom Heintjes, Benjamin Herman, John L.
Hone, Kevin Isaacson, William Insignares, Ed Jaster, Dale
Kelly, Vallerie Kelly, Bob Lesser, Paul Levitz, Larry Lowery,
Leonard Maltin, Harry Matetsky, Marc Nathan, Richard D.
Olson, Adam Philips, Jo Ann Reisler, Charlie Roberts, David
Robie, George Russell, Theresa Segreti, Maggie Thompson,
Paul A. Tiburzi, Tom Tumbush, Mort Walker, David Welch,
Doug Wheeler, John Zinewicz.

...And if anyone was inadvertently omitted, we
apologize and thank them for their input and support.

FOREWORD

BY JOHN K. SNYDER JR., PRESIDENT

First seen in newspapers, magazines, comic books, movies, radio or television, characters have made some of the greatest spokesmen the advertising world has ever witnessed. Each time a new form of media has emerged, fresh characters have sprung up and older, successful ones have been revived, helping to popularize products from juice, milk, other beverages, bread, cereal and candy to a dazzling array of consumer products. Through this process a wide range of characters has been instilled in the American psyche.

Their artifacts represent a major milestone in the histories of comic characters, children's education and entertainment, and marketing that closely parallels the history of this nation. The study of these benchmarks is intriguing in itself, as if we've been given the keys that unlock the mysteries of time and the spirit of childhood simultaneously.

From its earliest days, America has been driven by people who want to do better than the previous generation and in turn want their children to do even better than they had. Many of the toys you'll see represented in the museum are smaller versions of products originally aimed at adults. This has been a common pattern in toys through the generations. For example, first there were trains, then a few years later there were toy trains. Then there were cars and trucks, followed by toy cars and trucks.

While there certainly have been many toys simply geared toward entertainment, the most long-lived and successful types have been those designed not only to entertain but to educate, to speed along the process of socialization. Personal grooming, use of money, even job skills have been among the areas initiated or reinforced through the use of toys.

As you walk room by room through the museum, you'll be taken through a timeline that physically represents the intellectual thought behind that process. Instead of a stiff, theoretically dissection of marketing or training, you'll be treated to a visceral, lively presentation in which education and entertainment overlap to capture the imagination of young people.

Whether it was their favorite characters appearing on food products or other consumer products, children did indeed gravitate in many cases to creations that inspired them. As youngsters became young adults, some of that enthusiasm clearly stayed with them and served as the catalyst for their ambitions. Many scientists, aviators, doctors and others candidly give credit to the childhood inspirations of their adult successes.

This same motivation is evident in all the tremendous work that has been poured into the facility and into the pages of this book. Steve Geppi's personal vision for this museum has been made manifest in the rooms and halls of the museum, and it is a great reflection on all those who have toiled in this field over the centuries.

Preface
by Wendy Kelman, Executive Director

As Executive Director, I walk through Geppi's Entertainment Museum every day, and each time something new catches my eye! This book will allow you to visit the museum again and again, page by page. Although it by no means captures everything one can see at GEM, it can open the museum's doors to your friends and family to share a continuing exploration of American pop culture even when time does not allow for a visit in person.

When you do get the chance to visit in person, plan to stay for a day or several.... there's always plenty to see and do in Baltimore. You will have many opportunities to see each of the attractions highlighted in this book. Our interactive and changing exhibits will make each in-person visit a new experience.

If time allows, you may want to squeeze in a stop at an Orioles baseball game, or depending on the season, a Ravens football game. They are right around the corner as part of the Camden Yards complex. Stop into Sports Legends at Camden Yards, our downstairs neighbor where Babe Ruth and Cal Ripken share space with Johnny Unitas and many other icons.

Have more time? Consider including a short walk to the world famous Inner Harbor where shopping, dining and even boating abound, not to mention a variety of other attractions perfect for including in your trip to Baltimore and Geppi's Entertainment Museum.

The Museum is directly across the street from Baltimore's Convention Center (home of the Baltimore Comic-Con), a short ride from historic Fort McHenry, the Reginald F. Lewis Museum of African-American History & Culture, the National Aquarium in Baltimore, The Visionary Arts Museum or any number of other fine attractions, restaurants, and entertainment venues.

Too much to do in a single day? Absolutely! A multi-day visit will allow you to stay in one of our partner hotels, each of which will arrange a room and a trip to GEM (information can be found on our website, www.geppismuseum.com).

Start exploring Geppi's Entertainment Museum by way of this book, but come again in person, stay for a while and enjoy the continuing exploration of American pop culture.

Pop Culture With Character
by Dr. Arnold T. Blumberg, Curator

You're about to take a trip through time. There won't be any shiny brass machines to carry you through the ages, however; no chrome levers, no grinding temporal engines, no swirling mists as epochs race past your field of vision like wisps of forgotten memory. No, this journey will take place within your own mind and on the following pages as you step back with us to explore the rich history of the many characters that embodied American pop culture for the last 230 years.

Most of the events that shaped our world have been chronicled and interpreted many times over, but although we spend a lot of our time enjoying various forms of entertainment, we often have a dismissive view of its importance in the grander scope of history. Would we name Superman or Mickey Mouse in the same breath as Shakespeare or Einstein? Would we rank the works of Carl Barks or Jack Kirby alongside those of Michelangelo or Rembrandt?

Fortunately, this is not as strange an idea as it once was. Our attitude toward our own entertainment has changed significantly in recent years. We are now beginning to cast a more critical eye on the cultural elements that shape our identity as a people and a nation. The more we learn, the more we realize that the story of these pop culture characters is a familiar one that only changes on the surface. From the Brownies and the Yellow Kid to Spider-Man and SpongeBob SquarePants, these iconic figures touch us on a primal level by symbolizing our hopes and fears, our dreams and nightmares, our most devastating defeats and our greatest triumphs.

Our museum and this book pay tribute to all of these characters and the many books, toys and collectibles that remind us of a joke that made us laugh, an adventure yarn that thrilled us, or a smile that warmed our hearts. It's all about joy, pure and simple. Collectors in particular have a keen understanding of that joy. They slow down the inexorable flow of time by surrounding themselves with things that recall a childhood well spent in the land of dreams.

We hope you'll join us here in this book and at Geppi's Entertainment Museum to visit the past for a little while and then head back to the future where you can start or continue a collection of your own. After all...collecting builds character.

7

PIONEER SPIRIT

Play gives children a chance to practice what they are learning.
—*Fred Rogers*

The production and popularity of toys between 1776 and 1895 changed dramatically. Most toys were designed not only for entertainment but to teach children beliefs and values. Children were considered miniature adults, and most toys coached children in the ways of the adult world. More than just tools for escapism, toys were used to instruct children about the tasks required of them at present and in the years to come.

At first, children only played with toys sparingly and when not working, and only if the toy taught a moral lesson or biblical history. Toys reflected the times, whether it was wartime, peacetime, or the Industrial Revolution. Though a freer atmosphere evolved and toys were more widely accepted for fun as well as for education, they still often taught a lesson.

During this era, children played with homemade toys like cloth and straw dolls, or hand-carved wooden animals or vehicles, as well as manufactured playthings. Dolls reflected the fashions of the period and taught young girls how to prepare for parenting. Toy trains and boats imitated real world transportation and taught children about clockwork and steam mechanisms. Mechanical banks taught children how to save money. Marbles taught children about games of chance, counting and arithmetic. And the Brownies, the first commercially successful comic characters to endorse consumer products, generally featured a strong moral theme in their stories.

By the 1880s, the United States was on its way to becoming one of the largest producers of toys in the world, utilizing the abundant natural resources available to the nation—wood, tin and iron.

GEORGE WASHINGTON INAUGURAL CLOTHING BUTTON
Circa 1789. Unknown Mfg.

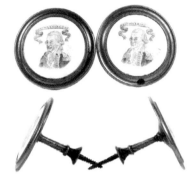

GEORGE WASHINGTON CURTAIN TIE BACKS
Circa 1800. Unknown Mfg.

THE GALLERY OF 140 COMICALITIES
1831. Bell's Life in London.

MAY THEY FULFILL THEIR PROMISES ILLUSTRATION BY JOSEPH KEPPLER
1879. Puck Magazine.

JOIN OR DIE SNAKE ILLUSTRATION BY BENJAMIN FRANKLIN
1754. The Pennsylvania Gazette.

Palmer Cox grew up in a region of Quebec steeped in Scottish folklore. He began his career by contributing poetry, prose and comic strips to various publications like *Wild Oats* and *The San Francisco Examiner* and became chief artist for *Uncle Sam: The American Journal of Wit and Humor* in 1875. But it was the introduction of his pixie-like Brownies in the pages of *St. Nicholas* magazine in 1883 that would make pop culture history in the early 1890s, bringing the twin forces of comic characters and character-based licensed merchandising together and setting the stage for an entire industry yet to come.

The Brownies were whimsical, fun-loving creatures inspired by Cox's memories of Scottish folktales. Though there were no female Brownies, they often represented particular occupations, such as the Policeman and the Sailor, or countries, like China, Ireland and Germany. The Brownies came about at a time when immigration was booming, and American children often identified with their favorite Brownie.

The Brownies' adventures always ended happily, often with an uplifting moral perspective. They had a positive influence on children and encouraged imaginative play, so it was no wonder parents agreed with giving their children toys that had a practical use. When the Brownies made the leap from the printed page to a wave of tie-in merchandise, children and adults were happily buying Brownies books, blocks, puzzles, dolls, printing sets and Kodak cameras for kids. The Log Cabin Brownies Biscuits became a favorite treat of children. All of these items enabled the Brownies to become the earliest recurring comic characters licensed to endorse products. The Brownies even starred in two plays, the second of which toured for five years after 100 performances in New York; both featured musical scores later offered to the public in sheet music.

As for Cox himself, he lived out the rest of his life in a custom-built home dubbed Brownie Castle. He died in 1924—his tombstone read: "In Creating the Brownies, He Bestowed a Priceless Heritage on Childhood."

BROWNIE NINE PINS BOWLING GAME
1893. McLoughlin Bros.

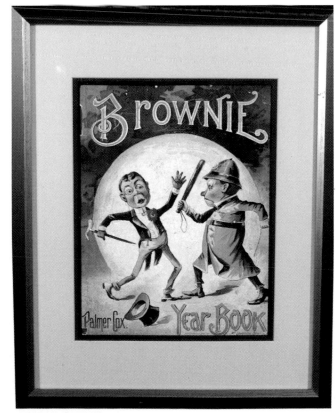

BROWNIE YEAR BOOK
1895. McLoughlin Bros.

BROWNIES CHEESE DISH
Circa 1890s. Unknown Mfg.

SET OF BROWNIES SPOONS
Circa 1890s. Unknown Mfg.

**POLICEMAN BROWNIE
CANDLE HOLDER**
Circa 1890s. Unknown Mfg.

BROWNIE CANDY CONTAINER
Circa 1890s. Unknown Mfg.

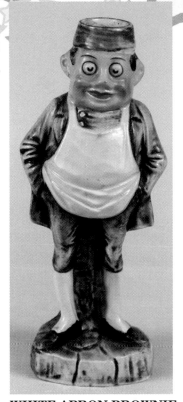

WHITE APRON BROWNIE CANDLE HOLDER
Circa 1890s. Unknown Mfg.

THE DUDE BROWNIE CANDLE HOLDER
Circa 1890s. Unknown Mfg.

Printing is one of the most significant achievements in history; the knowledge of printing brought with it the ability to readily reproduce and distribute information.

In the 1450s, German metalworker Johann Gutenberg invented a new type of printing press which used movable type. Prior to his invention, printing did exist but was limited in the number of editions that could be produced. The printing was engraved into wood, stone, or metal. Ink was rolled and transferred by pressure to vellum, with many of the books published during this time period being hand copied due to the limitations of the printing press.

Gutenberg's printing of the Bible was the first mass-produced book which not only revolutionized printing but also allowed for greater distribution of printed materials. The ability to easily duplicate information also opened the door to greater use of printed media both creatively and educationally, allowing artists and writers the chance to distribute their works to a much wider audience.

Early examples of comic art found in newspapers and books were only made accessible to the masses because of Gutenberg's printing press. As printing expanded into an industry in its own right, various editions of early Victorian Age comic books found their way into print in London, England and the United States of America. A medium had found its technology.

As part of society's effort to teach children about the world, toys often echo the tasks that we all must face when leaving childhood behind to face the harsher realities of daily life as an adult. Certainly one of the most important aspects of adult life is budgeting our money, and with a toy bank, children could get started right away.

Mechanical banks featured automatic mechanisms for moving and receiving coins, sometimes activated by the weight of a coin, but more frequently through the child pressing a lever, causing the coin to be dropped into the bank's hollow interior.

American companies J. & E. Stevens & Co. of Cromwell, Connecticut and Shepard Hardware Co. of Buffalo, New York, were the leading producers of cast iron mechanical banks. The first mechanical bank was the Hall's Excelsior by J. & E. Stevens & Co. in 1869. The American toy industry soon excelled in the production of cast iron toys, with mechanical banks forging a popular place in the market.

The intricate mechanisms of these banks sparked children's interest, encouraging them to save money as they pushed the lever again and again, enchanted by the clever action. Designers of the toy banks took the idea a step further and soon incorporated a variety of animal, occupational, ethnic, and biblical themes into their bank designs. Humor also became a common characteristic of most mechanical banks—one bank portrayed a mother eagle feeding her babies when her tail feathers were depressed, another featured William Tell shooting an apple off his son's head, and another had Jonah being thrown to a whale. Not only were these banks entertaining and educational, they even told a story through their precision-engineered action.

There are well over 500 documented antique mechanical banks that were produced prior to World War II. Though the earliest versions were made of wood, mechanical banks were also made of tin, aluminum and lead in addition to cast iron.

SNAPPING BULL DOG MECHANICAL BANK
1878. Ives.
Courtesy of Tom Sage, Sr. & Lori Sage

LION AND TWO MONKEYS MECHANICAL BANK
1883. Keyser & Rex.
Courtesy of John Morphy, M.D.

LEAP FROG MECHANICAL BANK
1891. Shepard Hardware Co.
Courtesy of Tom Sage, Sr. & Lori Sage

GIRL SKIPPING ROPE MECHANICAL BANK WITH BOX
1890. J&E Stevens.
Courtesy of Tom Sage, Sr. & Lori Sage

ARTILLERY MECHANICAL BANK
1892. J & E. Stevens.
Courtesy of Tom Sage, Sr. & Lori Sage

Tin is a soft and malleable metal, and tinplate is made when thin layers of steel or iron are dipped in molten tin. Tinplated sheets are then lithographed and stamped into whatever shape might be required. Although tin was used in early America for a variety of other uses, toys were often fashioned out of the leftover scraps. As tin toys increased in number and popularity, handmade and factory-produced wooden toys as well as playthings made of other native materials were rapidly displaced. The Industrial Revolution changed the character of our toys. Children were now able to acquire them at reasonable prices while design possibilities increased dramatically.

Early tinplate toys came from German companies like Bing, Fleischman, Lehmann, Gunthermann and Marklin. But it was in the United States where mass-production of tin toys began, giving birth to a long history of tin toy manufacturers. In 1838, the Philadelphia Tin Toy Manufactory—also known as Francis, Field, and Francis of Philadelphia—became the first toy manufacturer of record in America.

Other tinplate toy companies emerged by the 1860s, including the George W. Brown Co. of Connecticut, James Fallows and Co. of Philadelphia, and Althop, Bergmann and Co. of New York. Also founded in the 1860s, the Ives Co. of Connecticut is recognized mainly for toy trains. During the late 1860s and 1870s, toy factories turned out millions of tin toys, including horses pulling wagons, fire engines, animals, trains, boats and just about anything else that could be fashioned from tin. Most American tinplate toys had clockwork motors and performed various automatic actions as well.

In the late 1880s, European toy makers began to manufacture spring-driven toys that were much less expensive than their American clockwork cousins. Some of the most sought-after toys today were made from tin, including pull-along, clockwork, and wind-up toys of trains, boats, and animals.

HOSE REEL
1888. Wilkins.
Courtesy of Russ & Sheila Harrington

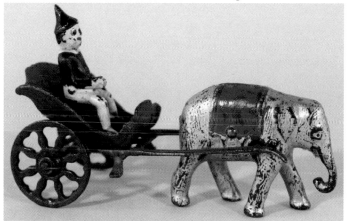

SET OF ANIMAL CARTS
Circa 1890s. Harris.
Courtesy of Russ & Sheila Harrington

TALLY-HO HORSE-DRAWN CARRIAGE
1883. Carpenter.
Courtesy of Russ & Sheila Harrington

LADDER TRUCK
Circa 1880. Carpenter.
Courtesy of Russ & Sheila Harrington

TWO SEAT SURREY
1892. Pratt & Lechtworth.
Courtesy of Russ & Sheila Harrington

GOAT CART
1880. Welker & Crosby.
Courtesy of Russ & Sheila Harrington

**PRESIDENT U.S. GRANT SMOKER
CLOCKWORK**
Circa 1880. Ives.
Courtesy of Bob Brady

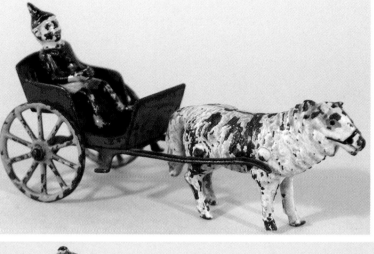

SET OF ANIMAL CARTS
Circa 1890s. Harris.
Courtesy of Russ & Sheila Harrington

21

THE EVOLUTION OF COMICS: PART 3

One of the important steps in the growth of visual storytelling and a key building block in the development of the comics medium was the word balloon. Modern comic strips and comic books may vary the design and placement of them, but word balloons are still closely related to those seen in the comics' earliest print predecessors, the broadsides. Some English magazines were even using them commonly by the 1780s.

Perhaps the earliest English language piece to employ word balloons was a *trompe l'oeil* or collage satirizing the catastrophic "South Sea Bubble," which dealt a severe blow to many investors in much the same way as the technology stock "New Economy" bubble would do in the 1990s.

The piece, titled "The Bubblers Medley, or a Sketch of the Times/Being Europe's Memorial from the Year 1720," includes a depiction of a number of men in a London coffeehouse, a typical place where merchants and others would gather to discuss the latest news; the men are speaking with word balloons surrounding their words. Other examples include a January 1799 foldout from *The Anti-Jacobin Review and Magazine* and the 1821 *General Satirist* cartoon, "A Consultation at the Medical Board."

The development and standardization of word balloon iconography in cartoons and comic strips continued through the eighteenth, nineteenth and early twentieth centuries.

Dolls made to resemble human beings have been a part of our culture almost since the beginning, and are often some of the most revealing artifacts for teaching us about aspects of our history. When humans fashion a facsimile of themselves, they invariably capture something about their beliefs, their feelings and their culture.

While many types of materials have been used to make dolls through the centuries, early fabric dolls were originally made at home to teach young girls how to sew and were assembled from rag, straw, wood, wax and cornhusks. The everyday actions of dressing, feeding and brushing a doll's hair prepared young women everywhere for the role of motherhood.

Developed in the 1800s, composition dolls were mixtures of pulped wood and paper that were molded under pressure. Frenchman Johann Maelzel invented speaking dolls in the 1820s, and dolls with moving eyes first appeared in England around 1825. Germany, France and Denmark started creating china heads for dolls in the 1840s that were then replaced by heads made of a more realistic-looking colored bisque in the 1860s.

The first American doll maker was granted a patent in 1840 and doll making became a bonafide industry in the United States after the Civil War in the 1860s. Celluloid was created shortly thereafter and dolls were soon mass-produced in large quantities. The finer examples were mostly made for wealthier children and royalty, and were imported from France and Germany. The demand for European fashion dolls expanded in the late 1860s and these too were imported from Europe to America.

Dollhouses offered a glimpse of home life in miniature. Early dollhouses were an extravagant luxury and only available to the rich. Though later dollhouses were perhaps not as elegant, they were more suitable for children from families with a wider range of income, and they provided endless hours of play.

JESTER DOLL & SIZE 3 PORTRAIT DOLL
Circa 1800s. Various Mfgs.
Courtesy of Connie & Jay Lowe

AUTOMATON WITH BASKET
Circa 1890s. Jumeau.
Courtesy of Connie & Jay Lowe

ANIMATED PULL TOY
1847. Unknown Mfg.
Courtesy of Connie & Jay Lowe

THE OLD WOMAN THAT LIVED IN A SHOE
Circa 1893. Ives.
Courtesy of Connie & Jay Lowe

SIZE 2 TETE DOLL
Circa 1880s. Jumeau.
Courtesy of Connie & Jay Lowe

SIZE 1 TETE DOLL
Circa 1880s. Jumeau.
Courtesy of Connie & Jay Lowe

DOLLHOUSE AND ACCESSORIES
Circa 1800s. Unknown Mfg.
Courtesy of Ann Meehan

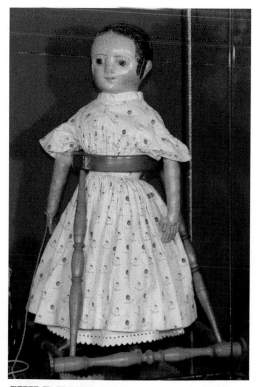

CHILD IN WALKER
Circa 1870s. German.
Courtesy of Connie & Jay Lowe

THE EVOLUTION OF COMICS: PART 4

Another one of the key building blocks in comics is the panel, an element without which sequential art wouldn't be so clearly defined. In a sense, all single-image cartoons are panels standing alone; the idea of placing individual narrative illustrations in order and using frames to separate them emerges solidly in the late 1800s in newspaper strips and comic supplements, sometimes with illustrations stacked in columns or loosely juxtaposed with no frames surrounding them.

Rodolphe Töpffer's *Obadiah Oldbuck* in 1842 is told in a series of paneled, captioned illustrations. George Cruikshank, J. Philip Cozans, Richard Doyle and Palmer Cox developed the concept by illustrating stories that split the narrative into numbered or at least sequential panels. By the time C.J. Taylor, F.M. Howarth and Gustave Verbeek were drawing strips for periodicals like *Puck*, *Judge* and *Truth*, the format was becoming formally established. Even then there were innovations like the unfurling panels in Hy Mayer's "Time, One Minute" in an 1896 issue of *Truth*.

Mark Fenderson is credited as the first artist to offer a sequence of comic pictures in a newspaper separated as nine specific panels. The January 28, 1894 piece is thus a watershed moment in the development of the modern American comic art form, but there are numerous other examples, many of which we are still discovering to this day.

With the discovery of steam power, the development of transportation technology accelerated rapidly throughout the end of the 1700s and well into the next century. The era of the steamboat began in America in 1787, and the first steam-powered locomotive was invented in 1801. American inventor Robert Fulton successfully built and operated an early submarine prototype in France, and by the 1870s, railroads had taken over as the major transporter of both goods and passengers. Public transportation quickly became an integral component of daily life, and of course, the toys of this time began to depict all of the vehicles that carried people to and fro.

Wooden trains and boats were produced in the 1850s and 1860s, but were soon replaced by cheaper tinplate versions, most of them manufactured in Germany and exported to the United States. By the 1870s, these tinplate toys had full clockwork and steam mechanisms—functioning miniature versions of their real world counterparts. The American-based toy companies such as Fallows, George Brown Co., and American Tin Company copied their German competitors and began producing comparable toys at home.

Importation of toys to the United States waned, and German companies like Marklin, Fleischmann, and Carrette answered the challenge by producing some of the most detailed and realistic toys of the time. Intricate works of art, these expensive toys could only be afforded by the wealthiest of families. The German manufacturers even began painting American names on the sides of these toys—for example, "The American" and "The New York."

Trains and boats were the most popular types of transportation being replicated as toys for children and adults alike to enjoy. These finely detailed, meticulously crafted toys are today considered to be the finest playthings ever made, a testament to their creators and the joy they brought to young and old.

NOAH'S ARK AND ANIMALS
Circa 1850. German.
Courtesy of Jim & Judy Konnerth

USS MONITOR
1870. George Brown.
Courtesy of Tom Sage, Sr. & Lori Sage

TRAIN SET
1881. Rock & Graner.
Courtesy of Tom Sage, Sr. & Lori Sage

1 GAUGE EAGLE TRAIN SET
Circa 1890s. Markin.
Courtesy of Tom Sage, Sr. & Lori Sage

3 GAUGE LIVE STEAM TRAIN SET
1885. Marklin.
Courtesy of Tom Sage, Sr. & Lori Sage

VICTORIA RIVERBOAT
1890. Marklin.
Courtesy of Tom Sage, Sr. & Lori Sage

HERTHA BATTLESHIP WITH HEYDE SAILORS
Circa 1890s. Bing.
Courtesy of Tom Sage, Sr. & Lori Sage

THE EVOLUTION OF COMICS: PART 5

The comic art form found much of its modern style and structure in those early years via illustrations that often commented on the politics of the era. These cartoons were typically satirical in nature and would illustrate different sides in the political topics of the day.

Political comics and cartoons could be found in publications like *Harper's Weekly*, the publication that featured Thomas Nast's well-known version of Santa Claus, or via the work of famous artist, silversmith and patriot Paul Revere, whose engraving of the broadside illustrating the Boston Massacre stands as a key early example of the art form. Other distinguished artists of the day included William Hogarth, George Cruikshank and Rodolphe Töpffer.

Using comics to comment on politics was a successful way to communicate to the masses at a time when many had a limited education. This was ultimately not just a form of entertainment but more importantly a way with which to educate people through narrative form.

Before the 1840s, the concept of visual art was limited to this form of narrative illustration, but when artist Louis Jacques Mandé Daguerre created the first easily-produced photographic process and went public in 1839, a new way to convey visual information to readers emerged to compete with hand-drawn comics. One might even say that the writing was on the wall.

29

Marbles are over 3,000 years old, part of a game that children around the world have been playing for millennia. Some of the oldest toys in human history, marbles were originally made of clay, bone, polished nuts and stones, and—appropriately enough—marble. Clay marbles have been found in ancient Egyptian tombs and references to marbles can be found in early Roman literature. Paintings and engravings often depict this popular pastime. Clearly, marbles have been a part of our heritage for a very long time.

However, it was not until 1846 when a German glass blower invented a device called marble scissors that marbles became extremely popular in both Europe and the United States. Initially intended for making glass eyes for animal toys, the scissors helped to mass-produce glass marbles starting in 1849-50, leaving behind telltale pontils where the glass was snipped from a rod. Later, glass marble manufacture spread to England and America, but German-made glass marbles remained sought after items.

The marble games played in the United States were variations of games that originated in England, where the British World Marbles Championship dated back to the 1600s. Games like Taw, Cherry Pit, and Nineholes were played with marbles like cat's-eyes, alleys and aggies. Marbles came in a wide variety of variations, colors and patterns made within the glass.

Different variations included chinas, lutzes, clambroths, swirls and sulphides. Sulphide marbles were clear with a clay animal or figure in the center, and introduced children to different animals. Marbles were primarily used to test one's skill at "shooting" or "knuckling down" and were also used to teach counting and arithmetic. Hundreds of years after American children first played marbles, the lingo lingers on. Before playing marbles, one must first decide whether to play for "keepsies" or just for fun.

TYPES OF MARBLES INCLUDE MICA, BLIZZARD, LUTZE, CHINA, CLAM, ONIONSKIN, END-OF-DAY, INDIAN, SULPHIDE AND SWIRLS
Circa 1880-1890. Various Mfgs.
Courtesy of Dan Morphy.

TYPES OF MARBLES INCLUDE MICA, BLIZZARD, LUTZE, CHINA, CLAM, ONIONSKIN, END-OF-DAY, INDIAN, SULPHIDE AND SWIRLS
Circa 1880-1890. Various Mfgs.
Courtesy of Dan Morphy.

TYPES OF MARBLES INCLUDE MICA, BLIZZARD, LUTZE, CHINA, CLAM, ONIONSKIN, END-OF-DAY, INDIAN, SULPHIDE AND SWIRLS
Circa 1880-1890. Various Mfgs.
Courtesy of Dan Morphy.

Before the Brownies merged the magic of comic characters with the power of character-based marketing, other early icons emerged that didn't enjoy the Brownies' success but paved the way for Palmer Cox's creations nevertheless.

American humor periodical *Brother Jonathan* introduced the nation to *Obadiah Oldbuck* in 1842, reformatting and reprinting a graphic novel by playwright, novelist and artist Rodolphe Töpffer. Another Töpffer creation, *Mr. Bachelor Butterfly*, made his debut in 1845.

In 1849, brothers James and Donald Read were inspired by Töpffer's work to introduce *Jeremiah Saddlebags*, a fellow out to get rich quick via the California gold rush. That historic influx of treasure-seekers also evidently included one *Mr. Tom Plump*, whose name accurately reflected his bulk; his adventures were chronicled by Philip J. Cozans in 1850.

Wilhelm Busch had his biggest success in the comics medium with two characters that later went on to enormous fame under another name. *Max and Maurice* debuted in 1871, and their mischievous shenanigans formed the basis for Rudolph Dirks' long-lived newspaper comic strip, *The Katzenjammer Kids*.

Even Cox himself presented a few other characters in the pages of *Wild Oats* prior to the Brownies' bow, including the couples of Mr. & Mrs. Sprowl and Bachelor Broke & Widow Snuggi.

While humans have been engaging in game play for about as long as they've existed, some of the card and board games we're most familiar with today date back only to about the 1700s, with card games like Solitaire being the first known in that particular category. Cartomancy—fortune telling with cards or tarot decks—began around 1765. Bridge was developed in the 1800s and poker was first mentioned in 1836. As for board rather than card-based games, *Snakes and Ladders* was published in England in the 1890s, and *Chinese Checkers* was published in 1892.

The first commercially produced American board game was *Mansion of Happiness*, developed in 1843 by S.B. Ives in Salem, Massachusetts. Good deeds moved players toward eternal happiness, while vices such as cruelty moved them backward. Most games produced at this time concentrated on education and fun, or taught moral and life lessons to the players.

Milton Bradley is credited with launching the modern game industry in North America. The company originally focused on lithography and printing, which later became useful as the graphics on games became more colorful and elaborate. Bradley invented the *Checkerboard Game of Life* in 1861, which emphasized reaching a happy old age over financial ruin. Milton Bradley and Company was formed in 1864.

George Parker invented his first game, *Banking*, when he was a teenager and published the game in 1883, inviting his brother Charles to join his game publishing company. Parker Brothers was established in 1888. By the late 1880s, Parker Brothers began advertising in newspapers and magazines, an unheard of practice at that time.

While board and boxed games were taking off in this era, wooden jigsaw puzzles were also popular. English engraver and mapmaker John Spilsbury marketed the first jigsaw puzzles in the 1760s as a set of eight maps that could be assembled to teach children about geography.

ASCENSION DE LA TOUR EIFFEL GAME
1889. Jumeau.
Courtesy of Connie & Jay Lowe

LITTLE GOLDENLOCKS AND THE THREE BEARS BOARD GAME
1890. McLoughlin Bros.

LITTLE GOLDENLOCKS AND THE THREE BEARS BOARD GAME BOARD AND SPINNER
1890. McLoughlin Bros.

THE EVOLUTION OF COMICS: PART 7

The road from the Brownies to the Yellow Kid is a short but interesting one as a medium found its footing and the notion of comic character-based licensing and merchandising took hold in a revolution that forever changed the way we view our entertainment and the products we buy.

When Cox created the Brownies, he may not have foreseen what was to come, but he established a template that others were eager to duplicate. Before Richard F. Outcault developed his seminal comic character, the Yellow Kid, others were testing the waters with characters and comic strips that eventually led to the introduction of the bald kid in the yellow nightshirt.

Outcault may have been partly inspired by the work of Michael Angelo Woolf, whose cartoons of slum-dwelling kids in *Life* certainly strike a familiar chord. Charles W. Saalburg had a cast of characters in *The Ting Ling Kids* that also recall that of Outcault's *Hogan's Alley*. Meanwhile, the first regularly recurring comic characters in newspapers were the *Little Bears* by Jimmy Swinnerton, appearing in the *San Francisco Examiner* in the early 1890s while not strictly starring in a strip of their own.

Outcault himself spent several years shaping the attributes of a character that would become a legendary figure in the annals of the comics medium; the Yellow Kid was about to arrive.

Extra! Extra!

Truth is not only stranger than fiction, it is more interesting.
—William Randolph Hearst

Americans in the late 1890s anticipated the next century with optimism. By 1900, only 35 years after the Civil War, America was transformed from a farm economy to fourth among industrialized nations. Rich resources, mass production and immigrant labor made prosperity not just expected but inevitable. However, one of eight Americans lived in poverty, child labor was rampant and corporations exploited with few consequences.

For many, the nation's economic rise meant more disposable income. Motion pictures and radio established a nationally shared popular culture. Newspapers introduced comic strips that educated as well as entertained and were easily shared between parents and children.

Childhood was recognized as a special phase of life separate from adulthood, and parents acknowledged the educational role toys play in teaching kids about the adult world. Toys with comic characters had more sales appeal than those without them.

In transportation, 15 million Model Ts had been manufactured by 1927. Giant steamships transported wealthy Americans to Europe and returned with millions of immigrants paying $10 (in 1904) for a new life. And following Orville Wright's 12-second 1903 test flight, one era ended and another dawned on May 20th, 1927, when Charles Lindbergh flew solo across the Atlantic, inspiring a generation and launching a national obsession with fictional flying heroes and superheroes.

SET OF THE GUMPS NODDERS
Circa 1925. Hertwig.

FOXY GRANDPA FIGURE
Circa 1900s. Unknown Mfg.

SON OF THE SHEIK LOBBY CARD
1926. United Artists.

YELLOW KID SCHOTTISCHE SHEET MUSIC
1897. Union Mutual Music Co.

THE NIGHT OF LOVE LOBBY CARD
1927. United Artists.

Immigrants poured into America during the 1890s. The streets of New York became a microcosm of the world, and the cartoons and illustrations of the city's newspapers provided a common language. The Yellow Kid was a child of those streets. Richard F. Outcault, his creator, dated the character's origin as 1892 and wrote, "I was drawing 'kid' pictures then, groups of street gamins of all sorts, and one day the Yellow Kid crept into one of those groups..."

Outcault sold his earliest "kid" cartoons to *Truth*, a weekly cartoon magazine in 1893. While still publishing in *Truth*, Outcault also began selling cartoons to Joseph Pulitzer's *New York World* newspaper in 1894. Little by little in 1894-1895, the bald-headed kid in the nightshirt emerged from the crowd in Outcault's *Hogan's Alley* panel cartoons.

The Yellow Kid's first appearance as a fully realized character, looking out at readers with his jug ears, prominent front teeth and yellow nightshirt was January 5, 1896 in the *New York World* panel cartoon, *Golf–The Great Society Sport As Played In Hogan's Alley*. On March 15, 1896, the Kid's nightshirt featured its first printed word, and in June 1896, he was first named Mickey Dugan. In October 1896, Outcault left the *World* for much higher pay at William Randolph Hearst's *New York Journal*.

Outcault's Yellow Kid was as much a social commentator as a comic character. Subjects ranged from sandlot baseball games to the 1896 presidential campaign. While many of the cartoons were large single panels, Outcault also drew cartoons with multiple panels and dialogue in word balloons, thereby claiming fame as the first true newspaper comic strip.

The Yellow Kid's appeal to adults resulted in brand name cigars, cigarettes and whiskey. For the children there were dolls, target games, cap bombs and chewing gum.

YELLOW KID FIGURE
Circa 1910s. Unknown Mfg.
Courtesy of Connie & Jay Lowe

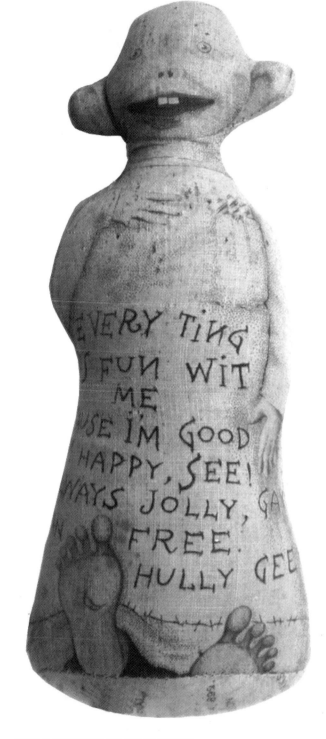

YELLOW KID CLOTH DOLL
1899. Arnold Print Works.

**AROUND THE WORLD WITH THE YELLOW KID
SUNDAY STRIP**
1897. New York Journal.

**DE YELLER KID'S
WHISKEY BOTTLE**
Circa 1896. Unknown Mfg.

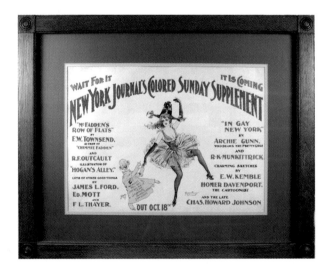

COLOR SUNDAY SUPPLEMENT DISPLAY AD
1896. New York Journal.

**YELLOW KID HIGH ADMIRAL
CIGARETTES BUTTON #88**
1896. Riley-Klotz M'F'G Co.

YELLOW KID ART
1898. George B. Luks.

A WEDDING IN HOGAN'S ALLEY SUNDAY STRIP
1897. The World.

SPOTLIGHT ON...
THE OTHER YELLOW KID

Joseph Pulitzer's *The New York World* and William Randolph Hearst's *The New York Journal* were fighting an intense legal battle against each other in the late 1890s for the rights to the Yellow Kid. Creator R.F. Outcault drew the Yellow Kid for *The World* until Hearst hired him away to draw the Kid for *The Journal*. Pulitzer countered by having George Luks, continue drawing the Kid for *The World*. Pulitzer retained the rights to the title, Hogan's Alley, under which Outcault began his strip. Outcault responded by moving the character in his Hearst-version of the strip to another neighborhood--McFadden's Row of Flats.

Luks' version of the Yellow Kid remained in his Hogan's Alley, and he had no problem moving the quarrel from the courtroom and taking it to the streets. His version of the strip took an overt dig at Outcault, having a character resembling the character creator sell cheap reproductions of the Yellow Kid and boasting them as "The Only Original Hogan." Despite Luks' clever insult, his version is often referred to as the "Other Yellow Kid."

Before long, both strips were re-named The Yellow Kid and the character's popularity far overshadowed the drama behind the scenes. Outcault returned to Pulitzer in 1898 to created a few small-time strips for the paper before breaking back into the iconic realm with 1902's Buster Brown. Luks left *The New York World* in 1900 to become a full-time painter, a medium for which he would become better known.

Richard Outcault's Yellow Kid was a child of the New York streets, but Outcault's next comic sensation, Buster Brown, was much the opposite. Buster was a child of wealth and privilege, sporting a pageboy hair style and decked out in fancy clothes.

With sister Mary Jane and pet terrier Tige, Buster provided Sunday comic readers with plenty of mischief and pranks. His "amusing capers" and "latest frolics" caused mayhem, but not dire consequences. Outcault's Buster was also approved by parents who a few years earlier considered the Yellow Kid unsuitable for children. Much of Buster's acceptance came from his "resolution panel" that concluded each strip; time after time, Buster apologized and "resolves" to improve his behavior.

Buster Brown first appeared in the *New York Herald* in 1902. His rise to national fame followed the 1904 World's Fair in St. Louis, attended by Outcault to license the use of the Buster Brown image on products. Buster endorsed everything from bread to stoves to cigars. Most notably, he became the trademark character for a line of shoes by the Brown Shoe Company—named for its founder, George W. Brown, not Buster. Promotions included a touring troupe of midgets appearing as Buster that visited theaters, fairs and department stores from 1904 into the 1920s.

Like the most popular characters, Buster soon expanded beyond the newspapers. His Sunday comics were among the earliest to be printed on better quality paper, bound in stiff cardboard illustrated covers and issued as tabloid-sized books— forerunners of the comic magazines of the 1930s. Buster had his own comic title distributed free by Buster Brown Shoes. Movie short subjects were released in the 1920s, and *The Buster Brown Gang with Smilin' Ed McConnell and Froggy the Gremlin* could be heard on radio and seen on TV from 1943 through 1954. Today, Buster Brown shoes still outfit infants to grade-schoolers.

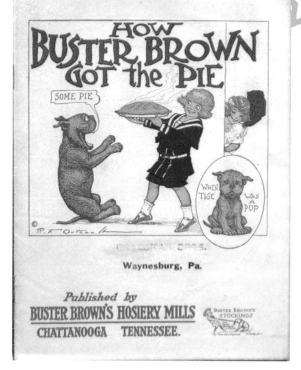

HOW BUSTER BROWN GOT THE PIE
Circa 1915. Buster Brown's Hosiery Mills

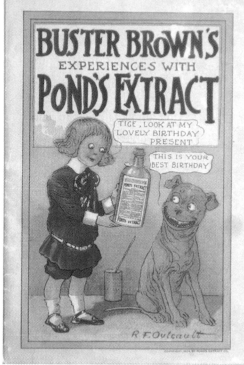

**BUSTER BROWN'S EXPERIENCES
WITH POND'S EXTRACT**
1904. Pond's Extract.

**BUSTER BROWN QUICK MEAL
STEEL RANGES**
Circa 1905. Kaufman & Strauss.

BUSTER BROWN TOOTHPICK HOLDER
Circa 1910s. Unknown Mfg.

SIGNED PHOTOGRAPH OF R.F. OUTCAULT AND DAUGHTER
Circa 1910s. Unknown photographer.

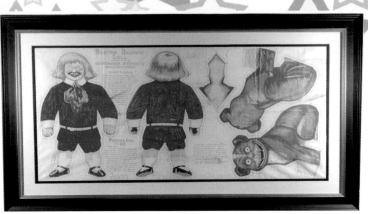

BUSTER BROWN AND TIGE CUT-OUT CLOTH DOLLS
Circa 1910s. Knickerbocker Specialty Co.

BUSTER BROWN'S AMUSING CAPERS COMIC BOOK
1908. Cupples & Leon Co.

BUSTER BROWN WITH THEODORE ROOSEVELT FRONT PAGE NEWSPAPER ART
Circa 1904. R. F. Outcault.

BUSTER BROWN VALENTINE
Circa 1910s. Raphael Tuck & Sons Co.

BUSTER BROWN CALENDAR POSTCARD
1914. Outcault Advertising Co.

PORE LI'L MOSE HIS LETTERS TO HIS MAMMY
1902. Cupples & Leon. Earliest Cupples & Leon comic.

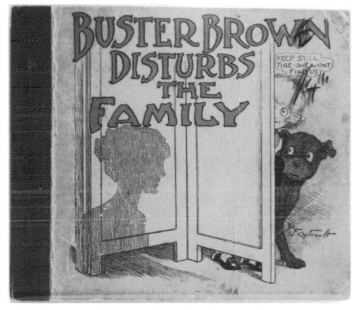

BUSTER BROWN DISTURBS THE FAMILY
1917. Frederick A. Stokes.

SET OF BUSTER BROWN BREAD CARDS
Circa 1910s. Unknown Mfg.

SPOTLIGHT ON...
PORE LI'L MOSE

The first ever newspaper strip to feature a Black protagonist, Richard Outcault's *Pore Li'l Mose* followed the exploits of a young African American boy as he left his rural hometown of Cottonville, Georgia for the northern, urban machine of New York City. By today's standards, the strip was decidedly politically incorrect with the "Cottonville" reference, Mose's charcoal skin, bugged eyes and thick lips perpetually puckered into an expression of alarm or surprise, and Mose's constant company of animals... including a monkey. There are also frequent references to his "letters to Mammy."

Despite these racial stereotypes, *Pore Li'l Mose* tells the fish-out-of-water tale of a boy in awe of his new, foreign and fast-paced surroundings – not uncommon comic fare. The Emancipation Proclamation wasn't even 40 years old when Outcault debuted the strip, and young Mose was consistent with public perception of Blacks in the early post-slavery era.

The strip only lasted a few years, experiencing its greatest popularity from 1901-1902. Mose was featured in his own books of strip art and even made appearances in early printings of Buster Brown books, but in later printings someone decided to replace Mose with the Yellow Kid. While the strip makes us cringe today, it's important to note that in 1901 it was considered revolutionary and nearly "sympathetic."

The term "science fiction" hadn't been invented when authors like Mary Shelley, Jules Verne, H.G. Wells and Edgar Rice Burroughs crafted fanciful adventure tales laced with intriguing speculation about Man's relationship with nature and technology. At the end of the 19th century, they were scientific romances, speculative fiction, and "scientifiction." Whatever the label, this literary genre blended fantasy, adventure and social commentary, capturing the imagination of American readers both young and old.

Shelley's *Frankenstein* (1818) is considered the first modern science fiction novel, a macabre tale of one inquisitive scientist delving too deeply into the secrets of life and death; lesser known is another Shelley work, *The Last Man* (1826), a post-apocalyptic story. Verne wrote extraordinary voyages that took readers on a *Journey to the Centre of the Earth* (1864), *From the Earth to the Moon* (1865) and *Twenty Thousand Leagues Under the Sea* (1869). Wells offered tales of *The Time Machine* (1895), *The Island of Dr. Moreau* (1896), *The Invisible Man* (1897) and *The War of the Worlds* (1898). And in 1912, Burroughs introduced an English lord turned primal jungle adventurer—Tarzan of the Apes; he also took another hero, John Carter, on a whirlwind trip to the red planet in *Under the Moons of Mars* (1912).

American science fiction found a home in anthology magazines like *Amazing Stories*, founded in 1926 by Hugo Gernsback. The August 1928 issue featured a man in a flying suit on the cover and the first Buck Rogers story inside, inspiring a generation of future authors and comic book creators. By the time Gernsback actually coined the term science fiction in 1929 in the pages of his next magazine, *Science Wonder Stories*, the visionaries named above had already provided readers with their own personal time machines, giving them a tantalizing glimpse of things to come and inspiring the architects of science fiction's golden age, including Isaac Asimov, Arthur C. Clarke, Ray Bradbury, and Robert Heinlein.

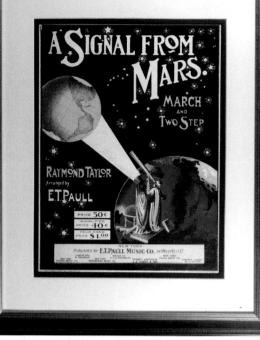

A SIGNAL FROM MARS SHEET MUSIC
1901. E.T. Paull Music Co.

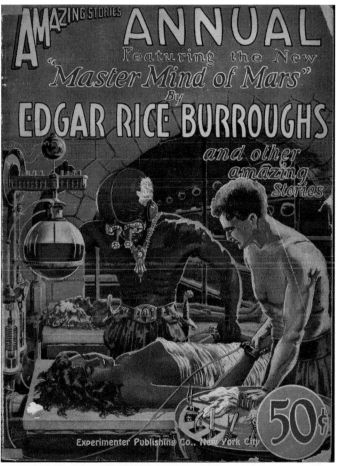

AMAZING STORIES ANNUAL VOL. 1 #1
1927. Experimenter Publishing Co.

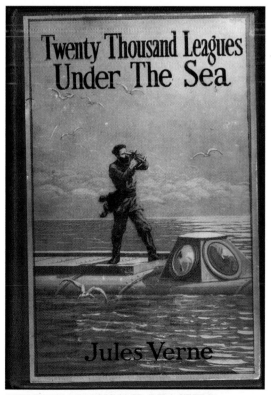

**TWENTY THOUSAND LEAGUES
UNDER THE SEA BY JULES VERNE**
1923. Charles Scribner's Sons.

DEN STORA MAGNETEN BY ANDRE LAURIE
1901. Hugo Gebers Förlag.

ELECTRICAL EXPERIMENTER #77
1919. Experimenter Publishing Co. Inc.

A WIERD THRILLING
ADVENTURE STORY,
EMBRACING ALL THE
FASCINATING ELEMENTS
OF SCREEN ROMANCE.
THE NEW YORK TRIBUNE
SAID-TARZAN OF THE
APES MUST BE SEEN TO
BE APPRECIATED

First Time at Popular Prices
15-20-30

RAY'S
Garden
OF PHOTOPLAY ART
MAIN AT NINTH

ONE WEEK ONLY
STARTING
Sunday, Jan. 26th

National Film Corp'n
of America
presents

TARZAN
OF THE **APES**

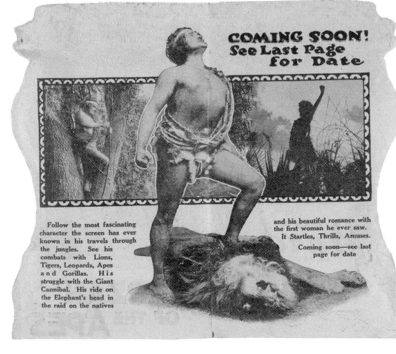

COMING SOON!
See Last Page
for Date

Follow the most fascinating
character the screen has ever
known in his travels through
the jungles. See his
combats with Lions,
Tigers, Leopards, Apes
a n d Gorillas. H i s
struggle with the Giant
Cannibal. His ride on
the Elephant's head in
the raid on the natives

and his beautiful romance with
the first woman he ever saw.
It Startles, Thrills, Amuses.

Coming soon—see last
page for date

TARZAN OF THE APES HERALD
1918. National Film Corp. of America.

SPOTLIGHT ON...
TARZAN

It began in 1912 when Edgar Rice Burroughs sold his adventure story, "Tarzan of the Apes – A Romance of the Jungle" to the pulp *All-Story Magazine*. The tale of an English orphan stranded in the depths of the African jungle and raised by apes captured the imagination of countless readers. In 1914, Tarzan leapt into novels and then film in 1918. The silent *Tarzan of the Apes*, starring Elmo Lincoln, became one of the first films to reach the million-dollar mark.

In the 1930s, as Tarzan appeared in newspaper strips and comic books, Johnny Weissmuller played the best remembered movie version of the character alongside Maureen O'Sullivan as Jane, starting with 1932's *Tarzan the Ape Man*. Tarzan also conquered radio in the first program of its kind to be pre-recorded on phonograph records; over 3,000 guests showed up at its Hollywood premiere. Promotions included games, figurines and buttons, and because the show was sponsored by Signal Oil Company for the first two years, cars were even running on Tarzan gas!

Burroughs died in 1951 but Tarzan lived on in more radio shows, comic books, television series, movies and endless merchandise. Today, Tarzan books are still in print, Dark Horse Comics continues his four-color exploits and Disney's 1999 animated feature film *Tarzan* met with huge success, including a Broadway production in 2006. The saga of the savage but noble Tarzan will likely never end.

William Randolph Hearst, successful publisher of the *San Francisco Examiner,* arrived in New York City in mid-1895. Hearst admired Joseph Pulitzer's *New York World,* but wanted his own New York best seller. Hearst purchased the *New York Journal* and cut the price from two cents to one cent, filling the Journal with content similar to the *World.* Circulation jumped but was far short of the *World*'s 500,000. Hearst's solutions came swiftly; with huge pay raises, he simply hired the *World*'s entire editorial staff and ordered a color press.

Pulitzer, understandably furious, cut his paper's price to one cent but tried to maintain revenue by increasing advertising rates. His advertisers rebelled by slashing ad placements. The two newspapers became locked in competition for decades.

In October 1896, Hearst struck again, hiring Pulitzer's star cartoonist Richard Outcault, the creator of the immensely popular Yellow Kid. When the legal dust settled, Pulitzer kept the strip's name–*Hogan's Alley,* now drawn by George Luks–but Outcault owned the character name copyrighted as The Yellow Kid.

In his book, *Yellow Journalism: Puncturing the Myths, Defining the Legacies,* historian W. Joseph Campbell cut through decades of misconceptions about the origin of the term "yellow journalism" and its possible inspirations, citing the Yellow Kid himself, the unethical reporting practices of the Hearst and Pulitzer newspaper organizations, and even an alleged "*Journal-Examiner* Yellow Fellow Transcontinental Bicycle Relay" created by Hearst in September 1896. The tug of war over Outcault's creation almost certainly played a role in *The New York Press* editor Ervin Wardman's decision to coin the term "yellow-kid journalism" in January 1897, later shortened to just "yellow journalism." The phrase is now synonymous with lurid, sensationalist and unscrupulous media tactics.

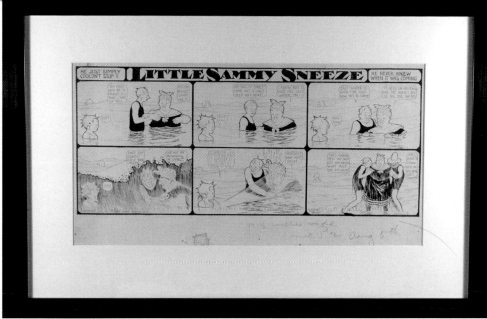

LITTLE SAMMY SNEEZE SUNDAY ART
1906. Winsor McCay.

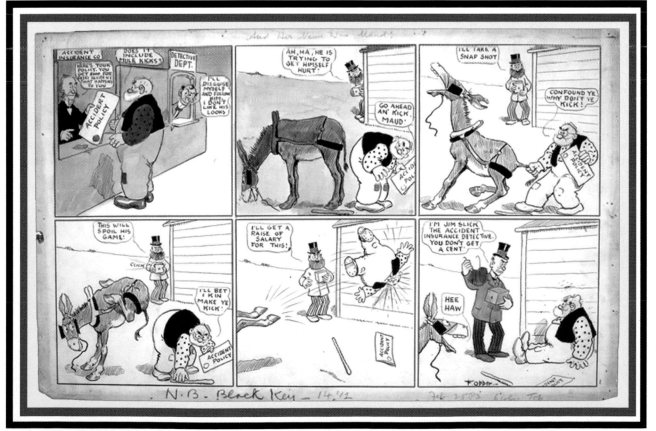

AND HER NAME WAS MAUDE! SUNDAY STRIP ART
1905. Frederick Opper.

THE REDS AND THE YELLOWS ILLUSTRATION BY JOSEPH KEPPLER JR.
1901. Puck Magazine.

WAR ILLUSTRATION BY VICTOR GILLAM
1898. Judge Magazine.

THE MUTT AND JEFF CARTOONS BY BUD FISHER
1910. The Ball Publishing Co.

MAMA KATZENJAMMER CANDY CONTAINER
Circa 1905-1915. Various Mfgs.

MAMA KATZENJAMMER TEA COZY
Circa 1905-1915. Various Mfgs.

SPOTLIGHT ON... THE KATZENJAMMER KIDS

The Yellow Kid wasn't the only one caught in the Hearst/Pulitzer crossfire. Rudolph Dirks' *The Katzenjammer Kids* was created in 1897 for *American Humorist*, the Sunday supplement of Hearst's *New York Journal*. Considered the first true color comic strip, it featured destructive twin brothers Hans and Fritz, their poor doting mother, ship-wrecked house-guest "der Captain" and dreaded truant officer "der Inspector."

When Dirks wanted to take a break in 1912, Hearst handed the strip to Harold H. Knerr, but when Dirks returned, Hearst refused to give the strip back to him. A court ruling awarded Hearst ownership of the strip while Dirks was allowed to use the characters elsewhere under a different title. In 1914, Dirks debuted *The Captain and the Kids* in rival Pulitzer papers while Knerr's version continued as *The Shenanigan Kids*.

The arrival of WWI inspired Knerr to lessen the strip's German references as the kids traveled around the world, eventually settling in the 'Squee-Jee Islands' in 1936. Many of the Knerr strip adventures closely paralleled the adventures Dirks had going on in his own strip.

Knerr died in 1949 and Dirks died in 1968 but the Kids continued to evolve with their German elements slowly filtered out through the years. The Katzenjammer Kids still make trouble today in one of America's longest-running comic strips.

Orville Wright turned fantasy into reality by flying for 12 seconds in a heavier-than-air machine at Kitty Hawk, North Carolina on December 17, 1903. His record lasted until later that afternoon, when brother Wilbur went aloft for 59 seconds.

Additional aviation milestones followed quickly. In 1909, Lieutenant F.E. Humphreys, after instruction from Wilbur Wright, became the first Army officer to fly solo in the Army's first airplane. The following year, the first airplane took off from the deck of a US warship. In 1911, the first cross-country flight was achieved; the air time was 82 hours, but it took Calbraith R. Rogers from September 11 until November 5 to get from New York City to Long Beach, California.

World War I inspired rapid advances in aviation technology, although American participation in the air war was largely limited to a few months in 1918. Captain "Eddie" Rickenbacker became the American "Ace of Aces," downing 26 German aircraft. Also in 1918, four experienced Army pilots and two recent pilot school graduates became the first group to fly air mail service between New York City and Washington, D.C.

In 1926, Richard E. Byrd and Floyd Bennett made the first flight over the North Pole. This was a prelude to Byrd's historic exploration of Antarctica and the South Pole beginning in 1928.

But of course, the paramount achievement in aviation during this era was accomplished by an unknown air mail pilot named Charles A. Lindbergh. His non-stop solo transatlantic flight from New York's Roosevelt Field to Orly airport outside Paris in his plane, the *Spirit of St. Louis*, was acclaimed worldwide. The Age of Aviation had begun in earnest.

Lindbergh's feat earned him superhero status throughout America and the world and inspired an entire generation's fascination with flying. "Lucky Lindy" and his amazing feat would shape the next two decades of pop culture as fictional flying heroes and superheroes took to the air.

FUTILE ATTACKS EDITORIAL ART
Circa 1910s. Winsor McCay.

UNCLE SAM ART
1911. Homer Davenport.

SET OF CHARLES LINDBERGH BUSTS AND BUTTONS
Circa 1927. Various Mfgs.

CHARLES LINDBERGH PENNANT
1927. Unknown Mfg.

CHARLES LINDBERGH RIBBON, BUSTS AND BUTTONS
Circa 1927. Various Mfgs.

SET OF PRESIDENTAL BUTTONS
1896-1924. Various Mfg.

CHARLES LINDBERGH POCKET MIRROR
Circa 1927. Unknown Mfg.

**CHARLES LINDBERGH
COMMEMORATIVE PLATE**
1927. Limoges China Co.

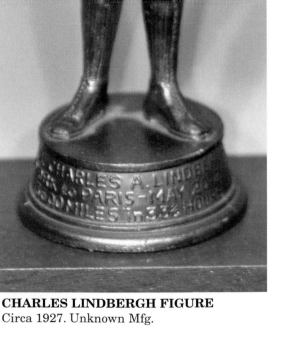

CHARLES LINDBERGH FIGURE
Circa 1927. Unknown Mfg.

59

1895 - 1927

Charles Lindbergh has been called the first international icon of the 20th century, credited with ushering in our current form of mass media treatment and our obsession with celebrities. The infamous kidnapping of his son in 1932 has also been responsible for infusing the Lindbergh name and legend with an air of mystery.

And yet, as remarkable as Charles Lindbergh and *The Spirit of St. Louis* were, he is also remembered as an uncomplicated person capable of extraordinary things, and a 25-year-old farmboy confident enough to take on a challenge simply by reason of being 25 and able to fly...and more than likely in need of the $25,000 award three pilots before him died trying to claim.

It's intriguing that an everyman claimed honor for pioneering a feat so tied to society's concept of superheroism. Ironically, in the years that have followed, very few receive that same honor for mastering the field he pioneered while flight remains among the favorite of all "superpowers" though its presence in everyday life has become so mundane.

Following his historic flight, Lindbergh plotted transcontinental air courses for TWA and served as an advisor to Pan Am. He also toiled to raise public awareness of environmental issues with little pomp or circumstance, and he was quietly devoted to his wife, Anne Morrow, until his death in Hawaii in 1974.

During the decade of the 1890s, around 10 million people made the safety bicycle their mode of personal transportation. With wheels of equal size, the safety bicycle could be balanced and ridden by anybody. In 1896, some 300 US factories enjoyed a $60 million dollar bicycle business.

Immense change, however, was just around the corner. On June 11, 1895, Charles Duryea received the first US patent for a gasoline driven car. A few months later, his brother Frank won the first US motor car race, 54 miles from Chicago to Evanston, Illinois and back.

From 8,000 registered cars in 1900 and only 150 miles of paved road, car ownership by 1916—aided by price decreases made possible by assembly line methods—stood at 3.5 million. By 1927, Henry Ford had produced his 15 millionth Model T.

On the oceans, massive steamships brought millions of immigrants to America's shores. The *Lusitania*, the largest ship in the world, made her maiden voyage in 1907 and set the record of 4 days, 18 hours, 40 minutes between Ireland and New York City. Panama Canal construction began in earnest in 1907 but the project wasn't completed until August 1914.

A catastrophe that would resonate for decades occurred in 1912 when the White Star Line's *Titanic* struck an iceberg and sank, with over 1,500 people losing their lives. Three years later, the *Lusitania* was struck by a German submarine torpedo with some loss of American lives. The US tried to remain neutral and didn't enter World War I until April 6, 1917.

Real cars and steamships inspired toy makers to produce elaborate and detailed replicas for children. Early on, the best quality tinplate toys came from Germany and England, but US toy makers quickly joined the market, broadening the materials used, the variety of replicas produced, and matching prices to the budgets of most parents anxious to provide their children with toys that replicated the adult world.

GIRAFFE CAGE
Circa 1906-1920. Hubley.
Courtesy of Russ & Sheila Harrington

TOURNEAU AUTO
Circa 1907-1908. Bing.
Courtesy of Tom Sage Sr. & Lori Sage

BAND WAGON
Circa 1906-1920. Hubley.
Courtesy of Russ & Sheila Harrington

1895 - 1927

PEDAL PUSH CAR
1927. Steelcraft.
Courtesy of Tom Sage, Sr. & Lori Sage

Thomas Edison's New Jersey movie studio—the Black Maria—made over 75 twenty-second films in 1894. Kinetoscope parlors sprang up nationwide. The first American audience to see a screen-projected movie gathered at Koster & Bial's Music Hall in New York on April 23, 1896, and a medium was officially born.

In 1903, director Edwin S. Porter pioneered movie story-telling with *The Great Train Robbery*, considered the first real movie as well as the first cowboy movie. By 1908, there were 8-10,000 nickelodeons, named for the 5-cent admission. They were often just a store front with one-reel movies projected on a bed sheet; daily attendance was about 200,000. The first two-reel feature film was D.W. Griffith's *Enoch Arden* in 1911. Cliffhanger serials began in 1912 and palatial movie theaters appeared in 1913.

The silent movie era's leading stars included comedians Charlie Chaplin and Harold Lloyd, leading ladies Mary Pickford and Clara Bow, leading men Douglas Fairbanks Sr. and Rudolph Valentino, "Man of 1,000 Faces" Lon Chaney, and cowboy Tom Mix, star of 300 films from 1910-1935.

While live-action movies flourished, animated movies made a slower but determined start. Winsor McKay's *Gertie the Dinosaur* enthralled 1914 audiences. Felix the Cat hit the screen in 1919 and reigned supreme among animated characters until a certain mouse took over in 1928. Walt Disney entered the animation field with *Alice's Wonderland* in 1924 and followed with a rabbit named Oswald in 1927.

Three landmark events occurred in 1927. *Wings*, with spectacular WWI aerial dogfight scenes, became the first feature film to win an Academy Award in 1929. At the same ceremony, Warner Bros. head Darryl Zanuck was presented a special Oscar "for producing *The Jazz Singer*, the pioneer outstanding talking picture, which has revolutionized the industry." That same year, the release of Fritz Lang's *Metropolis* inaugurated the science fiction film genre.

CHARLIE CHAPLIN WIND-UP
Circa 1920s. B&R.

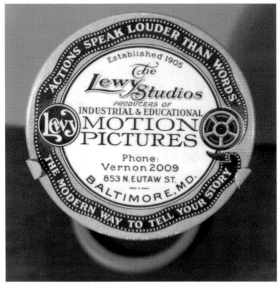

LEWY STUDIOS POCKET MIRROR
Circa 1920s. American Art Works.

KOKO THE CLOWN DOLL
Circa 1920. Schoenhut.

THE HAUNTED HOUSE ONE-SHEET
1921. Metro Pictures Corp.

FELIX THE CAT TOY CLOCK AND PITCHER
Circa 1920s. Various Mfgs.

FELIX THE CAT FROLIC PLATFORM TOY
1926. Nifty.
Collection of Michael Nemeth

Sometimes called the Charlie Chaplin of cartoon characters, Felix first emerged from the pen of Otto Messmer in 1919. He was by far the most popular cartoon character in the world before Mickey Mouse arrived, starting with *Feline Follies,* a five-minute short that was part of a Paramount Magazine serial release. His mischievous antics brought him international acclaim, especially in England.

In 1923, Felix began starring in his own King Features Syndicate Sunday strip, and the song "Felix Kept on Walking" became the biggest hit in London. Many of his short features were later edited to add sound in later years, and still others were distributed to television in 1953. In 1927, Charles Lindbergh even chose the hilarious cat to be the mascot of his transatlantic famous flight! 1927 was also the year Felix got his own daily strip, and the very next year, Felix became the first TV star.

In 1928, engineers at RCA were experimenting with television transmissions to a New York audience of about 150 television owners. Instead of an actor, the engineers used a 13" papier mache figure of Felix for the test broadcast.

Books, comic books and more movie shorts followed throughout the '30s. Messmer's assistant, Joe Oriolo, tweaked Felix's image and personality, also adding the cat's signature magic bag of tricks, as well as the Professor who wanted nothing more than to get his hands on that bag.

1895 - 1927

The story of food product advertising in the United States closely follows the arrival of the merchant class from Europe, where advertising had already taken hold. Things began simply with a wide variety of black and white advertising cards and pictorial labels, many examples of which from the early 1800s still exist. With the development of lithographic printing in the mid-1870s, however, there was an increase in the variety and styles of material produced.

After early advertising developed in chapbooks and handbills, one favorite means of conveying product information in the lithographic era was the trade card. Typically about three inches by five inches or smaller, these giveaway cards featured colorful scenes on one side, generally with a single color on the reverse and promotional text on one or both sides of the card. Although the cards were intended as advertisements, collecting and mounting them in albums was a popular hobby for many Americans. Many corporate names familiar today could be found on the trade cards of the 1870s-1890s, such as Borden's, Campbell's, Heinz and Swift.

In 1896, the invention of the celluloid pinback button joined the ranks of preferred promotional items for the nation's food makers. Also at this time, the popularity of trademarked and comic strip characters and the endorsement of food products by these characters took hold. Many characters designed exclusively to promote food products became popular icons in their own right. Aunt Jemima promoted the pancake flour of the R.T. Davis Mill & Manufacturing Company. Other well-known food product trademark characters created prior to 1928 are the Campbell Kids (1904), Mr. Peanut (1916), Sailor Jack (Cracker Jack, 1916), and Green Giant (1925).

In 1909, W.K. Kellogg was among the early cereal companies to offer kids a giveaway booklet, *Funny Jungleland*, hoping that children would influence their parents' purchasing choices. This marketing concept would blossom into the child-oriented premium industry of the early 1930s and beyond.

COCA-COLA DISPLAY SIGN
1914. Coca-Cola.

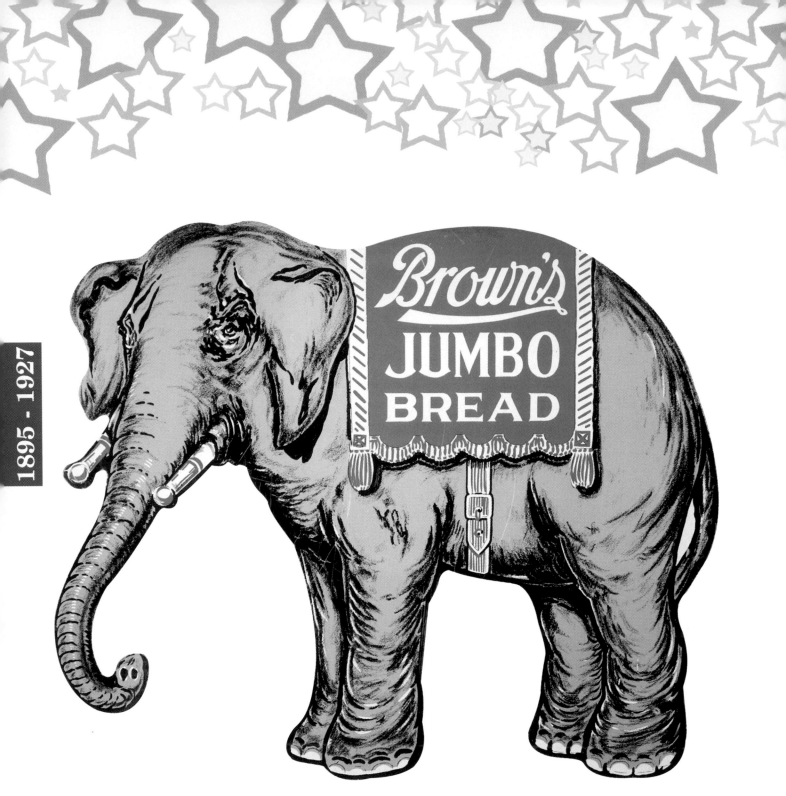

BROWN'S JUMBO BREAD DIE-CUT SIGN
Circa 1910s. Brown's Bread.

**MR. PEANUT CONVERTED BANK & SET OF
SWIZZLE STICKS**
Circa 1930-1970s. Planters.

SPOTLIGHT ON...
MR. PEANUT

An enduring part of our American culture, the Planters company has faithfully supplied our cocktail parties with assorted goodies for over a century. But in 1916, executives decided to host a contest to find a new company logo, and the Fred Astaire of food icons was born.

The search for the next peanut pitchman led executives to a young artist in a Suffolk, Virginia grade school. Thirteen-year-old Antonio Gentile submitted his contribution to the contest: a crude drawing of a peanut with arms and crossed legs. The contest judges excitedly hired a professional illustrator to give Antonio's sketch a bit more refinement, and he became a top-hatted, cane-wielding, monocle-sporting sophisti-nut.

The caricature Antonio named "Mr. Peanut" garnered the boy a "grand prize" of five dollars. While it *was* 1916, that seems a small sum since the dapper, dancing pip with his suave moves and peanutty pitches has undoubtedly made the company several fortunes over the years. Perhaps Planters could track down Antonio's family in time for Mr. Peanut's centennial in 2016 and duly compensate them for his adolescent labor of love?

Today Mr. Peanut is an American icon, especially on the Boardwalk in Atlantic City. In 1930, a Planters shop opened there with Mr. Peanut often on hand to greet visitors. In 2006, a statue of the character was installed across from the famed Boardwalk Hall.

The Yellow Kid proved to newspaper publishers that comics could build circulation and the floodgates opened as comic strips proliferated in the first quarter of the 20th century; a handful still run in papers today.

One of these, *The Katzenjammer Kids* (1897), was the first regular American feature to consistently use sequential panels. Creator Rudolph Dirks based his rambunctious twins Hans and Fritz on the 19th century German storybook characters Max and Moritz, favorites of *New York Journal* publisher William Randolph Hearst.

Pioneering strips included *Foxy Grandpa* (1901); *Buster Brown*, Richard Outcault's second major success in 1902; *Happy Hooligan* (1902); and *Little Nemo in Slumberland* (1906). By 1907, when Bud Fisher created the first successful strip to appear in daily newspapers, *Mutt & Jeff*, the hallmarks of the comic strip were established—a regular cast of characters, sequential panels and the use of word balloons.

Famous strips of the 1910s-1920s include *Krazy Kat* (1910), *Toonerville Folks* (1915), *Reg'lar Fellers* (1917), *The Gumps* (1917), *Bringing Up Father* (1917), *Barney Google* (1919), *Skeezix* (1921), *Just Kids* (1923), *Moon Mullins* (1923) and *Little Orphan Annie* (1924).

Syndicates such as King Features and the Chicago Tribune Syndicate were formed to distribute the strips to even the smallest newspapers throughout America. A farmer in Kansas and a bank teller in San Francisco could laugh at Irish tramp Happy Hooligan or prankster Buster Brown. Comic strip characters embodied the mass cultural experience we take for granted today. The most popular comic strip characters leapt off the newspaper pages and became three-dimensional toys and games, had their own specialized books, songs and sheet music, broke into the movies and crisscrossed America on the radio airwaves and in plays. The funny folks made a major impact on American pop culture and helped to create our national identity.

HAPPY HOOLIGAN DOLL
1924. Schoenhut.

FOXY GRANDPA SANTA CLAUS CUT-OUT
1902. New York American and Journal.

FUNNY FOLK CALENDAR
1906. New York Herald.

BRINGING UP FATHER DOLL SET
1924. Schoenhut.

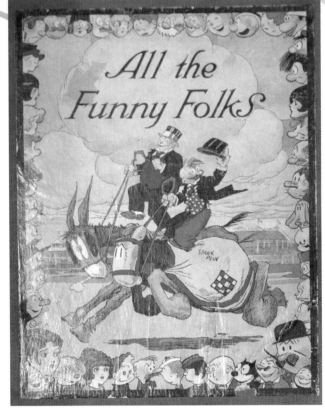

ALL THE FUNNY FOLKS BOOK
1926. The World Today Inc.

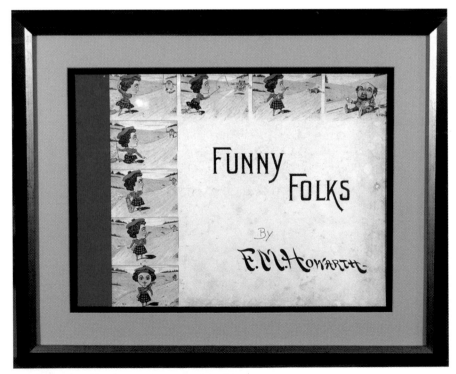

FUNNY FOLKS BY F.M. HOWARTH
1899. Dutton & Co.

74

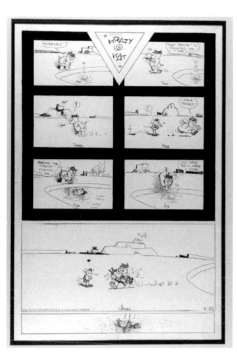

THE LAST KRAZY KAT SUNDAY STRIP ART
1944. George Herriman. The Herriman family states that this strip features the death of Krazy Kat.

LETTER OF SYMPATHY TO MABEL HERRIMAN FROM WALT DISNEY ON THE DEATH OF HER FATHER
1944. Walt Disney.

BARNEY GOOGLE PULL TOY
1924. Unknown Mfg.

SPOTLIGHT ON...
KRAZY KAT

Critically acclaimed as one of the most influential and sophisticated works of American pop art, George Herriman's Krazy Kat debuted in 1910 along with Ignatz Mouse and Offissa Pupp as part of a daily strip called *The Dingbat Family* (later *The Family Upstairs*). By 1913, Herriman had dropped the Dingbats and expanded *Krazy Kat* into a daily strip of its own, adding a Sunday page in 1916.

The strips have been dubbed visual poetry by luminaries like E.E. Cummings; a ballet was even created and staged in New York based on the strip. It was Herriman's ingenious use of vocabulary that was primarily responsible for this, along with a central bittersweet irony that made every Krazy adventure wonderfully bizarre.

Krazy Kat and Ignatz Mouse grew up together, and Krazy found himself (or herself, no one's really sure) 'krazy' for Ignatz, but Krazy's feelings were not reciprocated. The inevitable result of any interaction was Ignatz hitting Krazy in the head with a thrown brick. Krazy perversely interpreted these as gestures of affection, which outraged Ignatz all the more and forced Offissa Pupp to keep a special eye on him for Krazy's sake.

Herriman's sublime Art Deco artwork, deceptively simple plotting and profound emotional themes lent the strip an intellectual tone while keeping the material universally accessible, even to this day.

Believe it or not, gathering around a piano to play and sing popular songs was once a major pastime for American families, in an era before film, television, and even radio. In fact, the turn of the 19th century is dubbed the Golden Age of the Piano.

The sheet music employed in these social gatherings became accessible to many Americans as early as the 1820s. After the 1840s, covers with illustrations produced by lithography or chromolithography became economically feasible and made the music sheets graphically appealing.

As the music varied widely in style and theme, so too did the sheet music. With the rising popularity of parlor music in the 1860s, music types expanded to include minstrel songs, protest songs, sentimental songs, patriotic songs, political songs and much more.

By the 1890s, sheet music was so popular that it was frequently included as supplements to newspapers. Naturally, after 1895, comic strip characters became a major category for music publishers as the two met in newspapers and formed a perfect partnership. Many early newspaper comic strips and characters were adapted for production on the theatrical stage; examples include the Yellow Kid, *Foxy Grandpa*, *Little Nemo*, *Bringing Up Father*, and *Mutt & Jeff*. Every song in these stage productions could be published separately as an individual sheet music title.

Much of America's music and sheet music from 1885 into the 1920s originated in Tin Pan Alley. This was an actual block of 28th Street between 5th Avenue and Broadway in New York City. The name is attributed to newspaperman Monroe Rosenfeld and referred to the noise of many pianos coming from a multitude of music publishers' offices lining the street.

As the 20th century progressed, nearly every important event, person, movie star and comic character was documented and beautifully illustrated on sheet music.

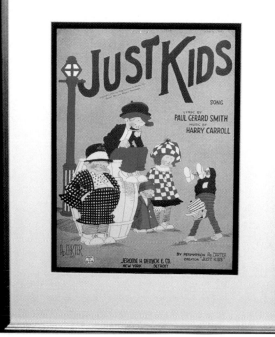

JUST KIDS SHEET MUSIC
1924. Jerome H. Remick & Co.

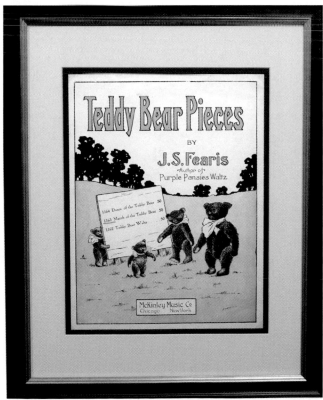

**MARCH OF THE TEDDY BEAR FROM TEDDY
BEAR PIECES SHEET MUSIC**
1907. McKinley Music Co.

1895 - 1927

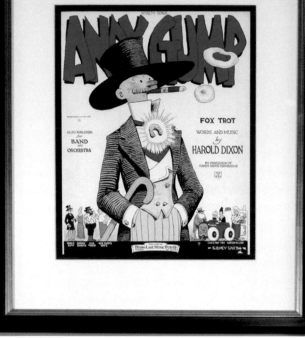

ANDY GUMP FOX TROT SHEET MUSIC
1923. Dixon-Lane Publishing.

BRINGING UP FATHER AT HOME SHEET MUSIC
1914. Harold Rossiter Music Co.

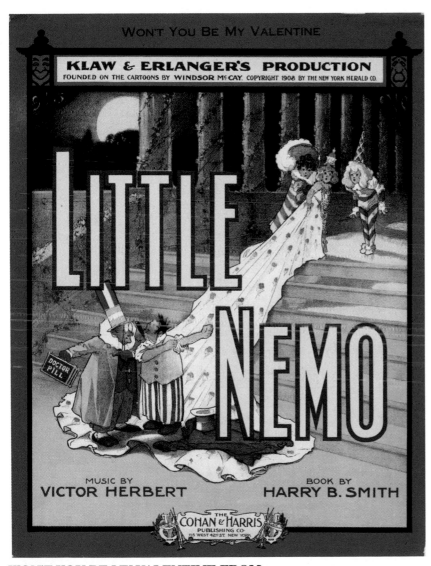

**WON'T YOU BE MY VALENTINE FROM
LITTLE NEMO SHEET MUSIC**
1913. Cohan & Harris.

SPOTLIGHT ON...
LITTLE NEMO

In 1908, Winsor McCay's Sunday comic strip, *Little Nemo in Slumberland*, took to the stage as a Broadway musical produced by the legendary Marcus Klaw and A.L. Erlanger, arguably the most powerful producers on Broadway during that time. Following the adventures of Nemo through the fairy-tale landscape of his dreams, the stage show featured the talents of writer Harry B. Smith, who produced the show book, and Victor Herbert (author of *Babes in Toyland*), who wrote the play and composed the show's score.

Whether on paper or stage, *Little Nemo in Slumberland* was a fantasy come to life. McCay's visionary journey into the world of dreams caught the imagination of children and adults alike. Fans came back week after week to see where Nemo was on his amazing journey to find Slumberland's Princess. Nemo's adventures always came up short when, at the end of each strip, he was yanked back to reality by waking up, often by his one-time enemy and sidekick, Flip (who wore a hat that said "Wake Up" on it).

The musical starred Joseph Cawthorne as King Morpheus and Master Gabriel as Nemo. Despite the expense of mounting such an elaborate production, the show was still quite successful and enjoyed a healthy run that began on October 20, 1908 with the final performance sending Nemo to sleep one more time on January 23, 1909.

When Heroes Unite

The only thing we have to fear is fear itself.
—*Franklin Delano Roosevelt*

All was prosperous. Herbert C. Hoover entered the White House declaring that poverty would soon be a thing of the past. Then the stock market crashed, the Dust Bowl dried out the southwest and the nation was plunged into the Great Depression.

Escape could be found in the comic pages, radio shows and movie houses. Popeye made his comic strip debut in 1929, as did Tarzan and Buck Rogers. Little Orphan Annie and Captain Midnight thrilled radio listeners. On the big screen, Mickey Mouse debuted in Disney's first talkie, *Steamboat Willie*, Shirley Temple captured America's hearts, and Fred Astaire and Ginger Rogers made the perfect team.

Franklin Delano Roosevelt was elected President in 1932, introducing a New Deal to stabilize the economy and restore national confidence. In 1937, Walt Disney Studios released *Snow White and the Seven Dwarfs*, their first full-length animated feature. The Golden Age of comics began with the debut of Superman in *Action Comics* #1. 1939 was considered the greatest year in cinema history with *Gone with the Wind*, *The Wizard of Oz*, *Stagecoach*, *Wuthering Heights* and *Mr. Smith Goes to Washington*.

On Dec 7, 1941, the Japanese bombed Pearl Harbor and the nation entered World War II. Americans found a vile foe in the Axis powers and soon the men, women, children, superheroes and cartoon characters of the Allied nations did their part for the war effort. In a time of heartbreak, death and destruction, America was united, heroic and victorious.

SET OF CAPTAIN MIDNIGHT MOVIE POSTERS
1942. Columbia Pictures.

WONDER WOMAN VALENTINE & BUTTON
Circa 1940s. Various Mfg.

THE FLASH BUTTON
1942. DC Comics.

**JUNIOR JUSTICE
SOCIETY BADGE**
1942. DC Comics.

BATMAN SCHOOLS AT WAR AD CARD
1943. United States Treasury Dept.

Smarting from the loss of his popular Oswald the Rabbit character and much of his staff, a young Walt Disney spent the better part of a railroad trip from New York to LA working on a new character–not a rabbit but a rodent. Disney had the perfect name–Mortimer Mouse. His wife thought otherwise and Mickey Mouse was born.

Working with Ub Iwerks, Disney spent six weeks co-directing Mickey and Minnie Mouse's first big screen adventure. On May 15, 1928, the duo debuted in *Plane Crazy*, with Mickey attempting to emulate Charles Lindbergh. Though it tested regionally well, the film did not secure a distributor. Disney and Iwerks tried again with *The Gallopin' Gaucho*, but lack of interest prevented its release. Disney needed something to make his character stand out; it was time to make Mickey talk.

Released on November 18, 1928, *Steamboat Willie* featured a synchronized soundtrack with Disney himself as Mickey. *Plane Crazy* and *The Gallopin' Gaucho* were re-released with added sound, followed by dozens of new adventures. Audiences were smitten with this new hero.

As his popularity grew, Mickey became less a prankster than a noble friend and role model to children. He was also a cultural phenomenon, with cartoons, books, comics, and feature films chronicling his exploits. His image appeared on glasses, dolls, buttons, masks, clocks, jewelry, milk bottles, lamps and cereal boxes. By the 1940s, Mickey was already a beloved American icon–an everyman, and by default, everymouse.

During World War II, the Nazis used images of Mickey Mouse to mock American culture, but the character survived and flourished. Decades later, President Jimmy Carter said it best: "Mickey Mouse is the symbol of goodwill, surpassing all languages and cultures. When one sees Mickey Mouse, they see happiness."

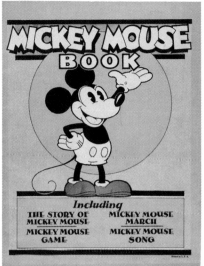

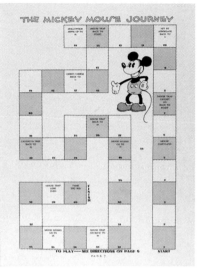

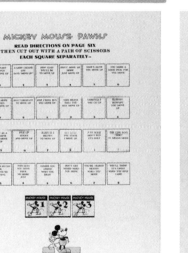

MICKEY MOUSE AVIATOR BADGE
Circa 1930s. Unknown Mfg.

1928 - 1945

MICKEY MOUSE BOOK
1930. Bibo and Lang.

A HANDFUL OF FUN BOOK
Circa 1935. Eisendrath Glove Co.

MICKEY MOUSE CLUB PATCH
1932. Fisch & Co..

MICKEY MOUSE CHORAL TOP
1934. Lackawanna Mfg. Co.

**MICKEY MOUSE
BUTTON AND DECAL**
Circa 1930s. Various Mfg.

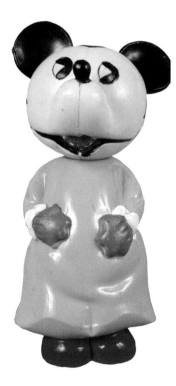

MICKEY'S NEPHEW FIGURE
Circa 1930s. Japan.

DONALD DUCK AND PLUTO PULL TOY
1936. Fisher Price.

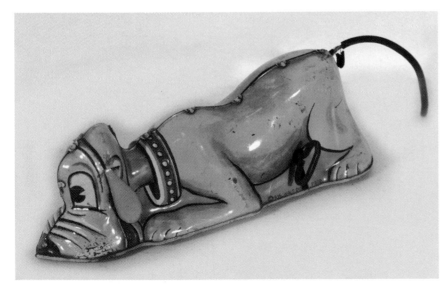

PLUTO WIND-UP TOY
1939. Louis Marx & Co.

Where would Mickey have been without his faithful pup, Pluto? The character made his first cartoon appearance in 1930, the same year that the planet Pluto was discovered (named after the Roman god, not the Disney dog). The energetic bloodhound was originally named Rover, but he got his new name in 1931. Some Disney historians assume that Pluto was renamed after the planet because of its prominence in the headlines.

Pluto debuted as a supporting player. His first starring roles came in the *Silly Symphony* shorts *Just Dogs* (1932) and *Mother Pluto* (1936). Then Pluto's own solo series began. Forty-eight theatrical cartoons were released from 1937 to 1953 After a thirty-five-year lull, eight more were produced for TV in 1999 and 2000.

Although Pluto is usually unable to speak English like his more humanoid co-stars, there have been exceptions. *The Moose Hunt* and *Mickey Steps Out* (both 1931) gave Pluto some dialogue, and *Mickey's Kangaroo* (1935) put a growly voice to his thoughts.

Pluto also debuted in the Mickey Mouse daily newspaper strip on July 8, 1931. He soon had comics of his own, the most famous being "Pluto Saves the Ship" in *Large Feature Comics* #7 (1942) – the first comic book work of Carl Barks. Ten years later, Pluto got his own feature in *Walt Disney's Comics and Stories*, written by Don Christensen with art by Paul Murry and Jack Bradbury.

The worldwide fame of Mickey Mouse inspired Walt Disney to be more audacious with his studio's output. Taking a suggestion from composer Carl Stalling, Disney developed *Silly Symphonies*, a series of musical cartoons. The first installment, *The Skeleton Dance*, was released in 1929, but when follow-ups didn't perform as well, Disney added a title card boasting "Mickey Mouse Presents a Silly Symphony."

Disney secured an exclusive contract for three-strip Technicolor and in 1932 released *Flowers and Trees*, the winner of the first Academy Award for Best Short Subject, Cartoons. Later that year the *Silly Symphonies* had their biggest hit with *The Three Little Pigs*. Featuring the hit single "Who's Afraid of the Big Bad Wolf?" the cartoon was followed by three other shorts featuring the pigs. More success followed with *The Grasshopper and the Ants* and *The Tortoise and the Hare*, featuring the alleged inspiration for Bugs Bunny.

In 1934, *The Wise Little Hen* marked the debut of a lazy lay-about named Donald Fauntleroy Duck that soon evolved into the familiar hot-headed little sailor and became Mickey's greatest rival for popularity. Donald joined with Mickey, Minnie and the former Dippy Dawg, now called Goofy, to firmly establish Disney in the minds of children.

In 1937, Disney released their first full-length animated feature film, *Snow White and the Seven Dwarfs*. It became the highest grossing film of 1938. Subsequent feature releases are remarkable for their longevity: *Pinocchio*, *Dumbo*, *Bambi*, and *Fantasia*.

Disney shifted his focus during the war years to boost morale at home and abroad. Donald Duck confronted Nazis in *Der Fuehrer's Face*, war bond purchasing was emphasized in *Seven Wise Dwarfs*, and a feature-length call for aerial dominance came with *Victory Through Air Power*. Disney provided educational films for troops and civilians designed to entertain as well as inform.

CONCEPTUAL ART FOR MUSIC LAND
Circa 1930s. Walt Disney Studios.

**JIMINY CRICKET
CONSCIENCE MEDAL**
1940. Schutter Candy Co.

1928 - 1945

"WHAT MAKES YER THINK SHE WANTS TO STAY?"

**CONCEPTUAL ART SNOW WHITE
AND THE SEVEN DWARFS**
Circa 1930s. Walt Disney Studios.

DUMBO MASK
1942. D-X Gasoline.

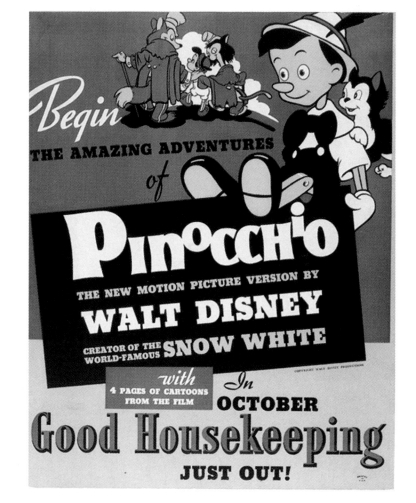

PINOCCHIO DOLL
1940. Ideal Toy Co.

GOOD HOUSEKEEPING DISPLAY SIGN
1939. Good Housekeeping.

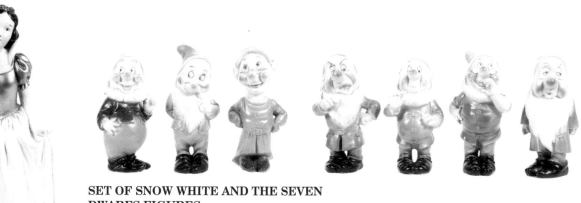

**SET OF SNOW WHITE AND THE SEVEN
DWARFS FIGURES**
Circa 1938. Leonardi Ltd.

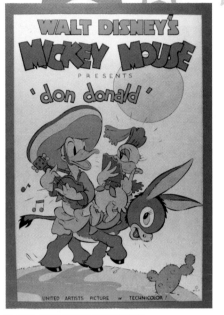

DON DONALD POSTER
1937. United Artists.

DONALD DUCK BUTTON
Circa 1930s. Walt Disney Enterprises.

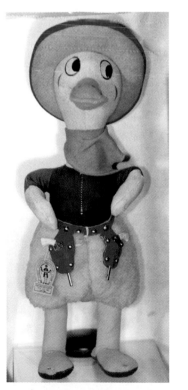

SET OF DONALD DUCK DOLLS
Circa 1930s. Knickerbocker Toy Co.

SPOTLIGHT ON...
DONALD DUCK

He's an angry everyman, the personification of the gutsy American spirit, and he has emerged as one of the most collected and documented comic characters in history.

Donald was first mentioned in the 1931 book, *The Adventures of Mickey Mouse* then again in *Mickey Mouse Annual* #3 in 1932. Both books picture a duck that may or may not be Donald; in the *Annual* he even has black feathers. Donald made his definitive first appearance in the *Silly Symphony* animated short, *The Wise Little Hen*, released in 1934. His second appearance in *Orphan's Benefit* saw him start to exhibit the angry, frustrated personality for which he would become so well known.

Donald entered the world of newspaper strips in 1934 with an adaptation of *The Wise Little Hen* for the *Silly Symphony* Sunday strip. Al Talliaferro became famous for drawing the strips, which he did until he died in 1969. It's also important to note Carl Barks' invaluable role in the shaping of Donald's character as well as the work of Clarence "Ducky" Nash and Dick Lundy, who served as Donald's voice and animator respectively.

As early as 1935, Donald was a balloon in Macy's parade, and 1936 saw the Victor Young orchestra record a hit dance tune about him. Donald's fiery temperament also made him a favorite icon to adorn airplanes and tanks during WWII. Today, Donald remains as endearing as ever, which we think is just ducky.

Disney was the animation king, but he was not without challengers. At Universal, Walter Lantz offered Disney's former character, Oswald the Rabbit, before achieving greater success with Andy Panda and Woody Woodpecker. Charles Mintz at Screen Gems/Columbia produced Krazy Kat and Scrappy cartoons. MGM produced *Happy Harmonies* and some of Tex Avery's finest work. Disney's chief animator, Ub Iwerks, left to open his own studio and created Flip the Frog.

Fleischer Studios existed nearly a decade before Disney and had already developed rotoscoping and combining live action with animation. In the '30s they released Betty Boop and Popeye cartoons while in the '40s they unleashed the animated adventures of Superman. An ill-advised attempt to challenge Disney on the feature front led to *Gulliver's Travels* and *Mr. Bug Goes to Town*, which failed to make a profit and resulted in the acquisition of the company by Paramount.

In 1930, Leon Schlesinger Productions presented the first *Looney Tunes* cartoon, *Sinkin' in the Bathtub*, which launched the mildly successful career of Bosko the Talk-Ink Kid. *Looney Tunes* were joined by *Merrie Melodies*, with both series intended as showcases for songs in the Warner Brothers library. When Bosko's creators Hugh Harman and Rudolf Ising left the studio and took Bosko with them, Schlesinger was left with the talents of animators Robert McKimson, Friz Freleng, Chuck Jones and Bob Clampett. The mighty men of "Termite Terrace"–a nickname for the Warner Brothers animation team–were assembled.

Tex Avery joined the team in 1936 and along with Bob Clampett generated the anarchic lunacy and exaggerated violence that defined the studio's output. Cartoon superstars emerged and Porky Pig, Daffy Duck, Tweety Bird and Bugs Bunny became household names. The rascally, rebellious antics of the *Looney Tunes* animators and their creations were a stark counterpoint to the established Disney style.

BETTY BOOP BUTTON
Circa 1930s. Parisian Novelty Co.

BETTY BOOP BRIDGE GAME
1932. Criterion Playing Card Co.

BETTY BOOP TEA SET
Circa 1930s. Geo Borgfeldt Corp.

PORKY PIG WIND-UP
1939. Louis Marx & Co.

GULLIVER'S TRAVELS PAPER DOLL CUT-OUTS BOOK
1939. Saalfield Publishing.

BUGS BUNNY CERAMIC
Circa 1940s. Shaw & Co.

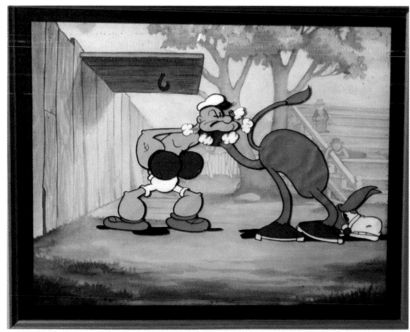

**LET'S YOU AND HIM FIGHT POPEYE ANIMATION CEL
AND PRODUCTION BACKGROUND**
1934. Max Fleischer Studios.

93

While Bugs Bunny was introduced in the 1940 cartoon "A Wild Hare," produced by Tex Avery and animated by Virgil Ross with a story by Rich Hogan and music by Carl Stalling, a similar rabbit appeared in cartoons four times before.

The 1938 cartoon "Porky's Hare Hunt" featured Porky Pig, Daffy Duck and a spunky rabbit crafted by World War I veteran Joseph "Bugs" Hardaway. In the 1939 cartoon, "Hare-um Scare-um," the hare in question was based on a model sheet by animator Charles Thorson. Thorson wrote the name "Bugs Bunny" on the sheet, but it's hard to say whether or not Thorson was joking with Hardaway.

When "A Wild Hare" came along, some speculated that Bugs' new appearance was inspired by Clark Gable. In *It Happened One Night*, Gable nonchalantly chomped on a carrot. Soon after, Bugs emerged with his trademark carrot as well as a pronounced mouth and strong jawline reminiscent of the dashing leading man.

Of course, Bugs wouldn't have been half the rabbit he became without the voice of versatile Mel Blanc, who blended a New York sound and sensibility with a Groucho Marx-like defiance of authority. Finally, Robert McKimson's revised model sheet in 1942 shaped Bugs' image into the wascally wabbit we know and love today. But with all these influences, Bugs has always been a true original. "Ain't I a stinker?"

1928 - 1945

Jerry Siegel and Joe Shuster were a writer/artist team struggling to find success with a strong man comic character inspired by newspaper strips like *Captain Easy*, *Buck Rogers*, *Flash Gordon*, *The Phantom* and *Popeye*, bodybuilder Bernarr McFadden, pulp adventurer Doc Savage (who by the way had a Fortress of Solitude), and a novel about eugenics by Philip Wylie, *Gladiator*. Siegel and Shuster's creation—an alien from a doomed world raised by Kansas farmers and possessed of a strong moral and patriotic fervor that leads him to adopt the guise of Superman—was a distillation of immigrant-fueled hopes of finding a place to belong, gaining acceptance, and achieving the American Dream. The two young men shared that vision with the world, and a hero was born.

Superman debuted in *Action Comics* #1 (June 1938), but he wasn't the all-powerful figure he would later become. For one thing, he didn't even fly; he leapt from place to place. For another, he was hardly the overgrown boy scout familiar to future generations, often employing more brutal tactics to defeat criminals, even if it meant the death of his foes. But for all the differences, some things were already in place—his banter with Lois Lane, his distinctive costume, and his unwavering devotion to truth, justice and the American way.

When *Action* and a companion comic book series, *Superman*, began selling in the millions, publisher Harry Donenfeld set up Superman Inc. just to handle the merchandising of their new hit hero. The Man of Tomorrow—later the Man of Steel—quickly migrated to radio, newspaper strips, movie theaters in the form of animated short features (and later, live-action serials), and a special "Superman Day" at the 1940 World's Fair, sponsored by Macy's department store.

By 1941, phrases like "Look, up in the sky" and "up, up and away" were familiar to audiences who thrilled to every new adventure of this strange visitor from a distant planet. In a few short years, Superman had become America's superhero.

SUPERMAN CARNIVAL STATUE
1940. Unknown Mfg.

SUPERMAN PICTURE PUZZLE
Circa 1940s. Superman Inc.

SUPERMAN SCHOOLS AT WAR AD CARD
1943. United States Treasury Dept.

SUPERMAN BELT
1940. Pioneer.

SUPERMAN VALENTINE
1940. Quality Art Novelty Co.

SUPERMAN RADIO SHOW AD
Circa 1940-1943. Force Cereal.

**SUPERMAN RADIO SHOW
CEREAL BOX AD**
1940. Force Cereal.

**SUPERMEN OF AMERICA
BUTTON**
Circa 1940s. DC Comics.

SUPERMEN OF AMERICA RING
1940. DC Comics.

CAPTAIN MARVEL FIGURE
1945. Multi Products.

CAPTAIN MARVEL FLIGHT CAP
1944. Fawcett Publications

CAPTAIN MARVEL SKULL CAP
1945. Fawcett Publications

SPECIAL EDITION COMICS #1 PRESS KIT
1940. Fawcett Publications.

SPOTLIGHT ON...
THE MARVEL FAMILY

Captain Marvel, the 'Big Red Cheese,' was just ordinary Billy Batson until he uttered 'Shazam' and became the World's Mightiest Mortal. He was already outselling Superman and rallying troops in the 1940s, but he was soon joined by allies in the battle against evil. Together they were the Marvel Family.

Billy's long-lost sister Mary became Mary Marvel in 1942's *Captain Marvel Adventures* #18 and even had her own fan club. While Billy's powers derived from six Roman gods, Mary's came from six goddesses whose names also lent their first initials to the magic word 'Shazam.'

In 1941's *Whiz Comics* #25, readers were introduced to newsboy Freddy Freeman, who was gravely injured in a battle with Captain Nazi. Captain Marvel and Mary Marvel imparted a portion of their powers to help him heal, and while Freddy himself remained crippled, he gained the ability to transform into Captain Marvel Jr. He later ventured outside the Marvel Family to work with The Crime Crusaders Club, which also featured Bulletman, Bulletgirl, and Minute Man.

Other Family members included the powerless Uncle Dudley, three Lieutenants Marvel that all shared the name Billy Batson, and even Baby Marvel! The unlikeliest member of the Family was Hoppy the Marvel Bunny, a statue of whom has become one of the most prized Captain Marvel-related collectibles.

Adventure, satire, slapstick, superheroes, talking animals, and vigilante cops–there was laughter and thrills every day in the newspaper strips and every month in the comic books. Moving gracefully into the era were established successes *Krazy Kat*, *Gasoline Alley* and *Little Orphan Annie*. The '20s ended with the first strip appearances of Edgar Rice Burroughs' *Tarzan*, illustrated by Hal Foster; Philip Francis Nowlan's *Buck Rogers in the 25th Century*; and Elzie Segar's *Thimble Theatre*, featuring the debut of Popeye.

The 1930s introduced single flapper Blondie Boopadoop in Chic Young's *Blondie*. *Dick Tracy* and *Secret Agent X-9* debuted, as did *Mandrake the Magician*. Alex Raymond sent *Flash Gordon* into space, and Al Capp took us to Dogpatch with *Li'l Abner*. Barney Google went down to Hootin' Holler and became buddies with *Snuffy Smith*. Lee Falk introduced *The Phantom*, while Hal Foster also offered the adventures of *Prince Valiant*.

In comic books, Bob Kane and Bill Finger gave the world Batman in *Detective Comics* #27. They were joined by Jerry Robinson as Batman was joined by Robin in *Detective Comics* #38. Jay Garrick inhaled chemicals that enhanced his metabolism in *Flash Comics* #1. In *Marvel Comics* #1, an American sea captain and an Atlantean emperor's daughter gave the world Namor the Sub-Mariner, while Professor Phineas T. Horton's android creation burst into flames, becoming the first Human Torch.

In the 1940s, Denny Colt was believed dead but Will Eisner brought him back as *The Spirit*. The Green Lantern first charged his ring in *All-American Comics* #16 and Fawcett Publications had their biggest success with Captain Marvel in *Whiz Comics* #1. Dr. William Moulton Marston decided that the superhero genre was lacking feminine power; under the pen name Charles Moulton, he premiered Wonder Woman in *All-Star Comics* #8. And lanky Private Steve Rogers, recipient of the experimental Super Soldier serum, was transformed into America's shield-slinging hero in *Captain America Comics* #1.

BLONDIE DAILY STRIP ART
1931. Chic Young.

SMOKEY STOVER SUNDAY STRIP ART
1936. Bill Holman.

**AMERICA'S GREATEST COMICS
CALENDAR**
1944. Chicago Herald-American.

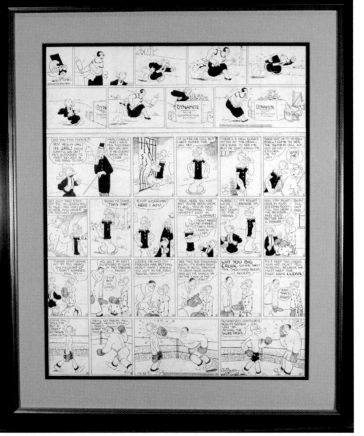

THIMBLE THEATRE SUNDAY STRIP ART
1930. E.C. Segar.

POPEYE PIRATE PISTOL
Circa 1935. Louis Marx & Co.

**SET OF DICK TRACY
BADGES AND CLUB KIT**
1938-1939. Quaker Cereal.

DICK TRACY CHARM BRACELET
1938. Quaker Cereal.

SPOTLIGHT ON...
DICK TRACY

Chester Gould was born in Oklahoma and eventually drew comics for the *Chicago Tribune,* but he was disturbed by the constant stream of unsavory headlines. In early '30s Chicago, crime was at its height, with gangsters making daily news.

Gould created a crime-fighting character named Plainclothes Tracy to try to combat the tide of violence and give children and adults a hero. He also created a rogues' gallery of villains, the first of whom was Big Boy, based directly on real-life mob king Al Capone.

The *Tribune*'s Joseph Patterson suggested changing the character's name to Dick Tracy (as many policemen were then nicknamed), and the strip debuted on October 4, 1931. The first sequence portrayed the kidnapping of Tracy's beloved Tess Trueheart and the killing of her father. This horrifying act, shown rather graphically in the strip, prompted Tracy to join the Plainclothesmen Squad and begin his lifelong quest to uphold justice. Within a few years the name Dick Tracy was the most recognized name in America.

Increasing popularity led to Tracy adopting a son named Junior, facing more fantastic villains like Pruneface and Flattop, and employing ahead-of-its-time gadgetry like Tracy's two-way wrist TV. Tracy was an early and successful transplant to the comic book format, and also turned up in radio, film and television as well as a plethora of crime-fighting collectibles.

Before the US officially entered the war, our nation's superheroes had already joined the fray, promoting patriotic devotion to the cause of liberty and justice and helping to "beat those Axis rats" on land, sea and air. And it wasn't just caped crusaders who duked it out with the likes of Hitler, Mussolini, and Tojo; funny animal characters like Donald Duck and Bugs Bunny were also donning military gear and striking a blow for freedom while touting war bonds.

Of course, having the comic characters fight our battles for us can open the door to uncomfortable questions about the difference between reality and fantasy. A child might wonder—if Superman is so powerful, why didn't he just fly over to the front and take out the Axis all by himself? Adults knew that kind of story could never be told, but it was up to parents to explain that to their children. In later years, DC Comics even invented a fantasy explanation involving Nazis dabbling in the occult for why the superheroes were unable to win the war on their own. But whether on the printed page or in the real world, there were limits to what our favorite comic characters could do.

Although Captain Marvel, Superman, the Shield, Wonder Woman and their colleagues couldn't bring the conflict to an end, they did help the war effort at home through their embodiment of America's fighting spirit. World War I pilots had inspired the creation of the fictional flying heroes, and the superheroes in turn galvanized a generation of would-be aviators who were ready when World War II arrived.

With their stark red, white and blue patriotism, unambiguous morality, and undying optimism, comic characters reassured the youth of a nation that victory was inevitable, that freedom and justice would prevail, and that the world would soon see the dawning of a new age. In America's darkest hour, our heroes united and led the way to a brighter, prosperous future.

ALL STAR COMICS #12
1942. National Periodical Publications.

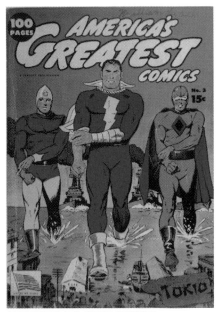

AMERICA'S GREATEST COMICS #3
1942. Fawcett Publications.

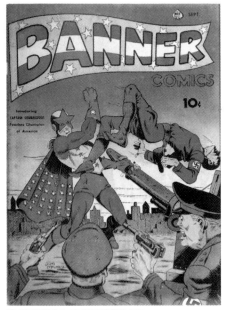

BANNER COMICS #3
1941. Ace Magazines.

1928 - 1945

CAPTAIN FLIGHT COMICS #1
1944. Four Star Publications.

CAPTAIN MARVEL ADVENTURES #21
1943. Fawcett Publications.

DAREDEVIL COMICS #1 (DARE-DEVIL BATTLES HITLER)
1941. Lev Gleason Publications.

Between the rapid growth of huge, impersonal cities, the looming specter of poverty, and the approaching terror of world war, American children in the 1930s and '40s needed more than ever to feel like they mattered, like they could make a difference...like they belonged.

The manufacturers of staple products—bread, milk and cereal—knew that children could form a strong foundation for their marketing efforts. They introduced clubs based on a variety of characters, newspaper strips and radio programs. Product mascots proliferated, offering children a chance to obtain exciting premiums and enjoy the real and psychological benefits of membership in something larger than themselves.

Secret pins, badges, insignia, handshakes, codes and club songs let strangers know that here was an individual with a dedication to drinking their Ovaltine and eating their Kellogg's, Post or Quaker cereal, thus advancing in the ranks of their chosen club. Available for box tops, proofs of purchase or the princely sum of ten cents were all manner of premium toys—hats, exclusive comics books, tommy guns, stickers, cut-outs and badges. A sought-after secret decoder pin could decipher a vital message on the Captain Midnight or Little Orphan Annie radio shows; a diligent club member could help their hero to save the world! Though most messages simply reminded loyal fans to consume the sponsors' products, there was always the hope that next time Buck Rogers would require their assistance, forcing them to eat their Cream of Wheat, leave their lunch pails behind and head off to the 25th Century.

Superman and the Justice Society recruited young Americans who proudly displayed their membership cards and certificates, while others received rings, pins and letters from The Shadow, Captain Marvel, Mary Marvel, Dick Tracy and the Lone Ranger. Clubs offered young fans a chance to connect with the characters they loved and with each other as well.

JR. DICK TRACY CRIME DETECTION FOLIO
Circa 1942. Miller Bros. Hat Co.

AMERICAN EAGLE DEFENDERS BUTTON
1942. Fox Features Syndicate.

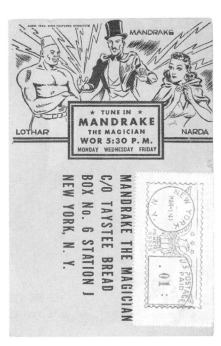

MANDRAKE THE MAGICIAN BUTTON AND APPLICATION CARD
1934-1941. Various Mfg.

Following Charles Lindbergh's flight across the Atlantic, America was swept up in an aviation craze. Daring pilots were national heroes and newspapers were filled with the exploits of Amelia Earhart, Floyd Bennett, Frank Hawks, Wiley Post and Howard Hughes.

On radio, World War I flying aces Robert M. Burtt and Wilfred G. Moore gave us *The Air Adventures of Jimmie Allen* and *Captain Midnight*. Jimmie Allen was a teenaged pilot who flew dangerous missions around the world. Captain Midnight was the undercover name for Captain Albright, who often matched wits with Ivan Shark and his daughter Fury. In 1940 he led the Secret Squadron and battled the evil Axis. Robert Hardy Andrews created *Jack Armstrong, The All-American Boy*, a show in the Frank Merriwell tradition that had an aviation angle. Comic character Hop Harrigan and his adventures with the All-American Aviation Company became a '40s radio staple.

Newspapers were filled with aviation-themed strips. Readers thrilled to the skybound adventures of *Tailspin Tommy, Skyroads, Smilin' Jack, Brick Bradford, Barney Baxter in the Air, Buz Sawyer*, and *Johnny Hazard*. In Milton Caniff's *Terry and the Pirates*, Terry Lee joined up with the Air Force during World War II.

The movies also took to the air. Though released in 1927, it was in 1929 that pilot turned director William A. Wellman's *Wings* took home the first Academy Award for Best Picture. Celebrated pilot and entrepreneur Howard Hughes gave the world spectacular dogfights and Jean Harlow in *Hell's Angels*. James Cagney took to the sky in *Devil Dogs of the Air*, and Errol Flynn did the same in *The Dawn Patrol*. Howard Hawks, another pilot turned director, dramatized the harrowing experience of mail pilots with *Only Angels Have Wings*, starring Cary Grant. The Duke himself, John Wayne, took flight in *Flying Tigers*, and Spencer Tracy starred in the story of the Enola Gay, *Thirty Seconds Over Tokyo*.

CAPT. SPARKS' TRAINING COCKPIT DISPLAY SIGN
1941. Quaker Cereals.

JR. BIRDMEN OF AMERICA PATCH, MEDAL AND MEMBERSHIP CARD
Circa 1930s. Hearst Newspapers.

THE MYSTERIOUS PILOT ONE-SHEET
1937. Columbia Pictures.

SET OF SKY CLIMBERS BADGES
Circa 1930s. Various Mfg.

LITTLE ORPHAN ANNIE ALTASCOPE RING
1942. Quaker Cereal.

AIR WARDEN CADET BUTTON
Circa 1943. F. C. Clover Co.

GRAF ZEPPELIN POCKET WATCH
Circa 1929. Westclox.

CAPTAIN MIDNIGHT DECODER BADGE
1942. Ovaltine.

SET OF JIMMIE ALLEN PATCHES AND STICKER
Circa 1930s. Various Mfg.

THE SKY PARADE LOBBY CARD
1936. Paramount Pictures.

The Air Adventures of Jimmie Allen aired from 1933-1942, and unlike some of his contemporaries, the high-flying, crime-solving, international air-racer was only 16 years old, practically a peer with his listeners.

The idea for this boy-pilot originally came from Bob Burtt and Bill Moore, two flying aces themselves. These WWI heroes piqued the interest of Russell C. Comer, who sold the idea to Skelly Oil. From there, things took off with the tale of messenger and pilot-in-training Jimmie at the Kansas City Airport. Forging a friendship with veteran pilot Speed Robertson and their mechanic Flash Lewis, Jimmie embarked on a series of dangerous missions, treasure hunts, enemy encounters, parachute jumps, emergency landings and sky-high adventures.

Jimmie's immense popularity inspired the creation of a Jimmie Allen Flying Club. Over half a million members received the club's weekly newspaper, as well as puzzles, cards, wings, emblems, patches, flight charts, and personalized letters from Jimmie himself. They could even pick up weekly flying lessons and model airplane kits at their local gas stations.

In 1936, Paramount Pictures released a Jimmie Allen movie titled *The Sky Parade*. This high-action, high-drama film was released at the height of Jimmie's popularity and featured Jimmie Allen playing himself.

1928 - 1945

113

The Wild West had long ago been tamed, but on the silver screen an audience could still experience an adventure from a time when the prairies needed crossing and a cowboy needed to do what was right or even burst into song. From pure escapism to social commentary, the minimalist settings of the early film westerns provided ample backdrop for an Indian ambush, a damsel in distress, and the potential evil of a man's soul.

Tom Mix, Buck Jones, Gene Autry, Roy Rogers, Dale Evans and William Boyd provided the Saturday matinee fare. Riding in from the silent era, Mix always dressed in splashy outfits, had a heart of gold and the strength of steel. Buck Jones twirled his gun through over 160 films. Gene Autry couldn't do the fancy cowboy tricks at first, but he could sing and quickly became "America's favorite cowboy." Roy Rogers, formerly Leonard Slye of the Sons of the Pioneers, was also a singer and rode into each adventure on his trusty stallion Trigger. 1944 saw a young Dale Evans pair up with Rogers for the first time in *Cowboy and the Senorita*. It was a successful pairing on and off screen. The duo soon married, becoming the first couple in westerns. William Boyd was intended to play the heavy in *Hop-a-Long Cassidy* (1935), but when the producers' choice for the lead declined, Boyd took that part instead. It was a perfect fit. Boyd went on to play Hopalong Cassidy in 66 westerns.

More mature westerns were helmed by auteurs like John Ford. Considered by many the finest American director, Ford was a sentimental storyteller with an eye for extraordinary imagery. His westerns are considered among the finest films ever produced—*Drums Along the Mohawk, Young Mr. Lincoln*—and he made John Wayne a star in *Stagecoach* (1939).

Born Marion Morrison, John Wayne was the personification of the western hero—larger than life and full of grit—but his star took a long time to rise. It wasn't until he was in his early 30s that he starred in *Stagecoach*. After that, he quickly became one of the greatest American heroes the movies ever made.

**SET OF TOM MIX BADGES WITH
WRANGLER PROTOTYPES**
1937-1938. Ralston Purina Co.

LONE RANGER DOLL
1938. Dollcraft Novelty Co.

SET OF TOM MIX WOOD GUNS
1933-1936. Ralston Purina Co.

Radio was ubiquitous in American homes during this era, inspiring families to gather around for the latest news, music, sports and original programming. America laughed at *Amos 'n' Andy*, *Fibber McGee and Molly*, *Baby Snooks*, *The Great Gildersleeve*, *The Edgar Bergen & Charlie McCarthy Show*, and *Burns and Allen*. Children hid under their sheets after hearing *Arch Oboler's Lights Out*, *Suspense*, and *Inner Sanctum*. Audiences thrilled to the exploits of *Little Orphan Annie*, *Doc Savage*, *Terry and the Pirates*, *Green Hornet*, *The Third Man*, and *The Shadow*. Kids enjoyed the storytelling of *The Singing Lady*. A variety of companies sponsored the shows each week.

Radio was king, but cinema was emperor. Hollywood gave America "more stars than there are in heaven." Epic escapism and social commentary exploded onto cinema screens; movie attendance reached an all-time high. Actors became America's royalty, with magazines offering the latest gossip on Fred Astaire, Ginger Rogers, Mickey Rooney, Mae West, Edward G. Robinson, Jackie Coogan, Wallace Beery, Clark Gable, Bette Davis, James Stewart, Jimmy Cagney, Joan Crawford, Katherine Hepburn, Shirley Temple and Cary Grant.

The Big Band sound ruled the dance halls with Benny Goodman, Henry James, Cab Calloway, Tommy Dorsey, Spike Jones, Glen Miller, and Duke Ellington. Jazz artists went mainstream as Louis Jordan, Ella Fitzgerald and Billie Holiday became hit parade favorites. Vocal artists like the Andrews Sisters, Dinah Shore, the Ink Spots, Bing Crosby and Frank Sinatra provided the soundtrack for World War II.

Sports teams gained nationwide popularity. Boxing enthusiasts marveled at Max Baer, Primo Carnera and Joe Louis; football fans thrilled to the Green Bay Packers, the Staten Island Stapletons and the Detroit Lions. Maintaining its hold on the hearts of Americans was the national pastime, baseball. From great teams came great men like Lou Gehrig, Dizzy Dean, Joe DiMaggio and Babe Ruth, all of whom had their own food-sponsored clubs.

SET OF FLASH GORDON PICTURE, CLICK GUN AND BUTTON
Circa 1936-1937. Various Mfgs.

BUCK ROGERS GIVEAWAY ILLUSTRATION
1929. John F. Dille Co. Cereal promotion.

CHECK AND DOUBLE CHECK WINDOW CARD
1930. RKO Radio Pictures.

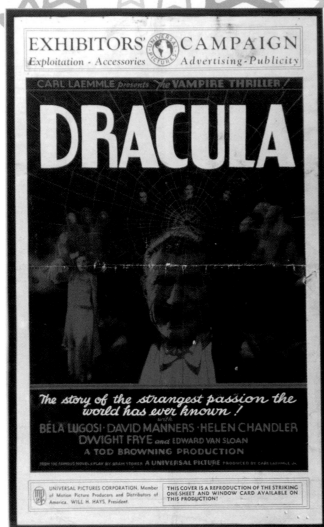

THE SHADOW RADIO SHOW DISPLAY SIGN
Circa 1934. Blue Coal and Shadow Magazine.

**SET OF DRACULA AND WEREWOLF OF LONDON
PRESS BOOKS**
1931-1935. Universal Studios.

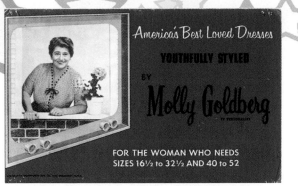

DRESSES BY MOLLY GOLDBERG AD
Circa 1950s. Wentworth Mfg. Co. Molly's popularity extended into the television era.

THE SHADOW PREMIUM CLUB PHOTO
Circa 1930s. Blue Coal.

SHIRLEY TEMPLE/DICK TRACY NEWSPAPER AD
1938. Quaker Cereal.

SPOTLIGHT ON...
THE GOLDBERGS

The first successful radio show to feature a Jewish family was written by, produced by and starred a woman. *The Rise of the Goldbergs* first aired on NBC radio in 1929. The creation of Gertrude Berg, the show chronicled the daily life of a working-class family in the Bronx. With the good-natured Molly as matriarch, the family became a quick hit with American audiences. The cast also included Jake (Molly's husband), children Sammy and Rosalie, and Uncle David.

Molly doled out wisdom and witticisms to her husband and kids for twenty-one years on three different networks (NBC, CBS, and Mutual). The series survived a name change to *The Goldbergs* in 1936 and a fictional location change from the Bronx to Lastonbury, Connecticut in 1939.

Berg kept cultural issues at the forefront of her pioneering series, centering many plots on World War II and its effect on America. In April 1939, an episode chronicled the interruption of the Goldberg's Passover Seder by a rock thrown through their living room window as news about Nazi Germany's advancement broke stateside. Other episodes featured news of family members or friends trying to escape Eastern Europe ahead of the Holocaust.

The Goldbergs also appeared in jigsaw puzzles, a comic strip (1944-1945), Broadway's *Molly and Me* (1948), a television sitcom (1949-1956), and a 1950 feature film titled *The Goldbergs*.

AMERICA TUNES IN

Say kids, what time is it?
—Buffalo Bob (Bob Smith)

Following World War II, Americans wanted peace and prosperity, and they got it–but not without a few bumps along the road. The US was now the paramount world power, but the Soviet Union soon ignored wartime agreements and the "Cold War" began. In 1957 the Soviets shocked America by launching the first space satellite, Sputnik, and the space race was on.

Jackie Robinson began the integration of major league baseball in 1947. On December 1, 1955 in Montgomery, Alabama, Rosa Parks was arrested for refusing to give up her bus seat to a white man. Dr. Martin Luther King led a non-violent boycott in response and became the spokesman of the civil rights movement.

By 1949, Americans were buying 100,000 television sets weekly, joining the shared experiences of a gigantic national audience. Howdy Doody was the king of children's shows, Captain Video was the first major sci-fi TV hero, and Hopalong Cassidy, the first successful TV western star, created a cowboy-themed merchandising phenomenon with several thousand licensed products.

Movies held their own with 2,000 drive-ins built from 1947-1950, and newspaper comic pages featured new strips such as *Pogo* and *Peanuts*. Aided by television, the "mood" music of the early 1950s was confronted mid-decade by the exuberance of rock and roll, named by disc jockey Alan Freed and personified by Elvis Presley, who has not left our building.

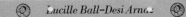

LASSIE DOLL
Circa 1950s. Smile Novelty Toy Co.

LUCY & DESI DIXIE PUBLICITY PHOTO
Circa 1953. Dixie Ice Cream.

**ELVIS PRESLEY PUBLICITY
PHOTO AND FRAME**
1956. Elvis Presley Enterprises.

A TRIBUTE TO JAMES DEAN LP
1956. Columbia.

**MICKEY MANTLE AND
ROGER MARIS BUTTONS**
Circa 1950s. Unknown Mfgs.

Every Baby Boomer born between 1947 and 1960 could answer *Howdy Doody Show* host Buffalo Bob's question: "Say kids, what time is it?" with an enthusiastic "It's Howdy Doody Time!" By January 1950, television was in 3 million American homes and comic-inspired characters were at the forefront. All the puppet shows–*The Howdy Doody Show*, *Foodini The Great* and *Kukla, Fran & Ollie*–were at heart comic characters brought to life on the small screen, and Howdy Doody was the undisputed king of the puppets. Robert "Buffalo Bob" Smith created the character and hosted the show. Millions of kids joined the in-studio Peanut Gallery to enjoy the antics of Doodyville residents that included Clarabell the Clown, Indian Princess Summerfall Winterspring and Howdy's marionette friends Mr. Bluster, Dilly Dally, and Flub-A-Dub.

The early *Puppet Playhouse* shows–the series' original title–were largely commercial free, but that was about to change. Writer Eddie Kean, inspired by the 1948 presidential election, decided Howdy should run for President of the kids. Howdy asked kids to write him with ideas for his campaign platform and thousands of letters arrived. Producer Robert Muir received permission to offer 10,000 campaign buttons reading "I'm For Howdy Doody" as mail-in premiums. The free button announcement was first made March 23, 1948; only five stations were airing the show and the offer was made seven times. NBC executives were astonished when 60,000 requests rolled into the mailroom. This simple giveaway button became the first television premium for kids and the overwhelming response demonstrated the immense appeal of the show. Colgate, Continental Baking, Ovaltine and Mars Candy quickly signed on as sponsors.

Howdy's success led to a daily comic strip, Dell comic books and a radio version of the show. Howdy proved the appeal of comic characters on the small screen and the influence of children's programming on parents' purchasing choices.

HOWDY DOODY BUBBLE BATH
Circa 1951. Champrel Co.

DOIN' THE HOWDY DOODY WIND-UP
Circa 1948-1951. Unique Art Mfg. Co. Inc.

HOWDY DOODY SIPMUG WITH BOX
Circa 1950s. Century Plastic Co.

HOWDY DOODY BUTTON
1948. Unknown Mfg.

1946 - 1960

PRINCESS SUMMERFALL WINTERSPRING DOLL.
Circa 1950s. Beehler Arts Ltd.

HOWDY DOODY DOLL
Circa 1947. Effanbee Doll Co.

HOWDY DOODY SOUVENIR TAG
1950. Blue Cross.

126

HOWDY DOODY RECORD PLAYER
Circa 1950s. Shura-Tone.

HOWDY DOODY SIGNAL FLASHER RING
Circa 1950s. Brownie Mfg. Co.

Kukla, Fran and Ollie was the first TV puppet show to be equally popular with kids and adults. Though it first aired on NBC in 1948, the premise predated the series by nearly a decade. Creator Burr Tillstrom's Kuklapolitan Players first appeared at the 1939 New York World's Fair. Kukla and Ollie provided festival commentary, heckled announcers and interviewed celebrities. Tillstrom improvised over 2,000 performances at the Fair. The Players also entertained at USO shows during WWII. There, Tillstrom met Fran Allison.

In 1947, Chicago network executives contracted the Kuklapolitans for thirteen weeks that turned into an entire decade on air, first as an hour show then later as a half hour and then fifteen minutes. In its heyday, over six million viewers tuned in, and the cast received nearly 15,000 letters a day. The show was formidable competition for other televised powerhouses of the day, like *The Ed Sullivan Show* and *The Milton Berle Show*.

When Kukla, Fran and Ollie finished its original run in 1957, fans lamented the loss, sparking a brief 1961 revival. Fran was absent and the format was only five minutes! Nearly a decade later, the show was revamped for PBS and ran from 1969 to 1971. At the end of its PBS renaissance, the troupe began to crop up on CBS as hosts for its Saturday Children's Film Festival. They remained there until 1979.

1946 - 1960

The advent of commercial television in 1947 sparked an entertainment revolution. Early television shows reflected and affected family life in the '50s—women were homemakers, fathers knew best and the kids were spunky but ultimately obedient. Families watched and imitated *I Love Lucy*, *Father Knows Best* and *The Adventures of Ozzie and Harriet*. *Dragnet*'s Sgt. Joe Friday taught that crime doesn't pay. Radio, vaudeville and nightclub comedians like Milton Berle, Ed Wynn, Jack Benny, Burns and Allen, Jackie Gleason and Sid Caesar moved to television, providing comedy for the entire family.

Fears that sporting event attendance would suffer proved unfounded. Three months after Brooklyn Dodger Jackie Robinson broke the major league baseball color barrier in 1947, Larry Doby became the first black player in the American League by joining the Cleveland Indians, who in 1948 drew 2.5 million fans, the largest crowd ever at that time.

While television actually created event-attending fans, the movie industry suffered a reversal of fortune. In 1947, average weekly attendance was ninety million; in 1950, it fell to sixty million. Even gimmicks like 1953's *Bwana Devil* 3-D feature, with spears and lions hurtling at the audience, couldn't stop the slide, which dropped to forty million weekly in 1957.

The peacetime prosperity of the 1950s made teenagers an economic and social force hungry for their own identity. Rock 'n' roll owes a lot to the blues; James Brown, Little Richard and Elvis Aaron Presley found the formula to deliver the message to America's teenagers. In 1956, sixty million people—82.6% of the television audience—watched Elvis' appearance on the *Ed Sullivan Show* and made him the king of the teen idols that followed.

Unlike many radio shows with a single sponsor, the increased costs of television production required shared sponsorship, usually by makers of food products such as cereal, bread and candy. Show-related giveaway toys remained popular through the 1950s all the way up to the present day.

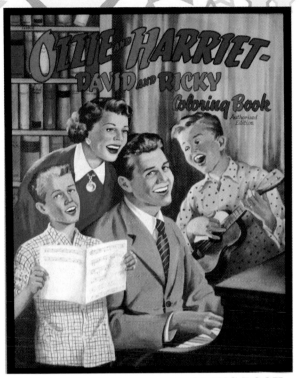

OZZIE AND HARRIET COLORING BOOK
Circa 1950s. Saalfield Publishing.

DRAGNET BADGE
1955. Sherry TV Inc.

FROGGY THE GREMLIN SQUEEZE TOY
1948. Rempel Mfg. Inc.

DRAGNET PUZZLE
1955. Transogram Co. Inc.

1946 - 1960

CAPTAIN KANGAROO PUPPET THEATER
Circa 1950s. Rushtime.

MARY HARTLINE DOLL
Circa 1950s. Ideal Toy Co.

130

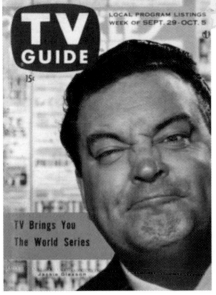

TV GUIDE SEPT. 29-OCT. 5
1956. Triangle Publications Inc.

MY LOVE SONG TO YOU SHEET MUSIC
1954. Song Smiths Inc.

JACKIE GLEASON BUS
1955. Wolverine Supply and Mfg. Co.

You would think that with its success in various media before and after its debut as its own television series, *The Honeymooners* would have enjoyed a long run on the small screen. However, the show only lasted one season (1955-1956) on CBS. Jackie Gleason first launched the legendary foursome – his own Ralph Kramden and wife Alice (Audrey Meadows) with neighbors Ed and Trixie Norton (Art Carney, Joyce Randolph) – on Gleason's first variety series, *Cavalcade of Stars*, in 1951.

The Honeymooners were an anomaly for television in the 1950s. Shows of the time generally featured couples and families in middle- and upper-middle-class brackets, while *The Honeymooners* followed the money-making schemes of a working-class Brooklynite (Ralph) and his savant neighbor, Ed. There was constant bickering of the loud variety, not the gentle differences of opinion common to the shows preceding it, and reconciliation so last-minute viewers may have wondered if it would occur before the credits rolled.

Despite its short run, *The Honeymooners* is among America's most beloved series. Gleason continued performing sketches featuring the characters in his subsequent variety shows, replacing cast members when necessary. The last of the Honeymooners appearances starring Gleason aired in the late 1970s. The show continues to enjoy strong viewership in syndication. "Baby, you're the greatest!"

1946 - 1960

131

After World War II, Walt Disney converted his production facilities from making military training films to commercial features. *Make Mine Music* and *Song of the South* were released in 1946. Major releases of the 1950s included *Cinderella* (1950), *Alice In Wonderland* (1951), *Peter Pan* (1953) and a trio of Davy Crockett films in 1955-1956 that followed on the heels of the first Disney television show.

Disneyland (later *The Wonderful World of Disney*) aired October 27, 1954 on ABC while the first Disneyland theme park opened July 17, 1955 in Anaheim, California. Both the show and park promoted Disney characters. 1955 saw Davy Crockett mania reigning supreme among America's youngsters.

Eager to capture a late afternoon children's audience, ABC brought *The Mickey Mouse Club* to television on October 3, 1955; the club had first formed in 1929 to promote theatrical cartoons. The show's stars were a group of children known as Mouseketeers who were about the same age as their audience. Kids were encouraged to wear the official Mouseketeer hat, a black beanie with Mickey ears. By year's end, Mouseketeers Annette Funicello and Cubby O'Brien were household names and Benay-Albee Novelty Company had shipped 550,000 beanies. By early 1956, the show had 16.5 million viewers and a huge selection of licensed merchandise on store shelves.

The Mickey Mouse Club didn't just sell Disney merchandise. Mattel sponsored three commercials daily for a year, defying the conventional wisdom that toys were purchased only by adults at Christmas. Mattel's success inspired other companies to follow suit, taking the first steps toward a year-round toy market. Other sponsors included Pillsbury, Welch's, Mars and Ipana Toothpaste, whose animated spokesman Bucky Beaver had everyone singing "Brusha brusha brusha/Get the new Ipana."

For four years the Mouseketeers sang and danced, and all of America knew the words to the show's theme song: "Who's the leader of the club/That's made for you and me/M-I-C-K-E-Y/M-O-U-S-E!"

FANTASYLAND BOARD GAME
1956. Parker Brothers.

MICKEY MOUSE ROLLER SKATES
Circa 1950s. Globe-Union Inc.

1946 - 1960

**MOUSEKETEER "JAY JAY" SOLARI'S
TALENT ROUNDUP COWBOY COSTUME**
Circa 1956-1957. Walt Disney Studios.

DISNEYLAND LUNCHBOX
Circa 1950s. Aladdin Industries.

MICKEY THE MAGICIAN BATTERY OPERATED TOY
Circa 1950s. Line Mar Toys.

134

ANNETTE FUNICELLO PAPER DOLL
1958. Cheerios.

SPECIAL DEPUTY MOUSEKETEER BADGE
Circa 1950s. L.M. Eddie Mfg.

Annette Funicello gained Mouseketeer stardom way before the days of Britney, Justin and Christina, and with a last name that begins with "fun" it's no wonder she quickly became America's sweetheart.

Personally chosen by Walt Disney when he saw her dancing in a production of Swan Lake, Annette could also sing and act and radiate the wholesome appeal that made the 13-year-old an instant MMC fan favorite. It wasn't long before she even had her own series within the Club, *Annette*. She was consistently featured in teen magazines, and was the ultimate positive influence on other teens.

The end of *The Mickey Mouse Club* did not spell the end of Annette's popularity. Annette remained under contract with Disney and appeared in a variety of Disney television shows and feature films, including *Babes in Toyland* and *The Shaggy Dog*. She was still under contract with Disney when she began appearing in her kitchy, campy beach party movies with Frankie Avalon. Amid all the bikini clad, boy-crazy gals and surfing musclemen, Annette perfectly maintained her wholesome image. Her fame was furthered with the recording of dozens of Top 40 songs, such as "Tall Paul" and "Pineapple Princess."

Annette's popularity continued long after her contract with Disney was up. Decades later, she is still a household name - the perfect all-American teenager.

1946 - 1960

Buck Rogers and Wilma Deering were the first successful space-traveling comic strip characters. Their daily newspaper adventures began in 1929 and a radio show debuted in 1932. They were joined by another comic strip starring Flash Gordon and Dale Arden in 1934. On television, *Captain Video and his Video Rangers* were first to venture into the solar system, premiering on the Dumont network in 1949. The show had a meager budget but enthralled young viewers with futuristic devices like the Radio Scillograph and Cosmic Ray Vibrator—props fashioned from cardboard and household items.

Taking the video space race to the next level was *Tom Corbett, Space Cadet*. The live broadcast began on CBS in 1950 but also aired on ABC, NBC and the Dumont network before ending in 1955. Corbett's exploits were distinguished by their scientific accuracy, provided by rocket scientist Willy Ley. Kellogg's cereal offered several dozen premiums but the show was also extensively licensed to toy makers who filled stores with space-themed equipment ranging from two-way phones to space goggles.

The ultimate space adventure of the 1950s was *Space Patrol*, debuting locally in Los Angeles in March 1950; six months later it went national on ABC, airing until 1955. The show followed the adventures of Commander Buzz Corry and Cadet Happy as they policed galaxies in their spaceship Terra V for the United Planets of the 30th century. Kids could enact their own *Space Patrol* adventures with toys like the Lunar Fleet Base, Cosmic Smoke Gun and Outer Space Helmet. Some licensed toys offered in connection with the show were largely available only on the west coast.

These three space-themed shows of the early 1950s were all essentially devoted to law and order with an underlying theme of peace in the atomic age. They provided young viewers with a glimpse of actual space exploration that became reality just a few years later.

TOM CORBETT SPACE CADET CLUB KIT
1951. Kellogg's.

SET OF TOY SPACEMEN FIGURES
Circa 1950s. Thomas Toys.

TOM CORBETT SPACE CADET SPACE GUN
Circa 1950s. Louis Marx & Co.

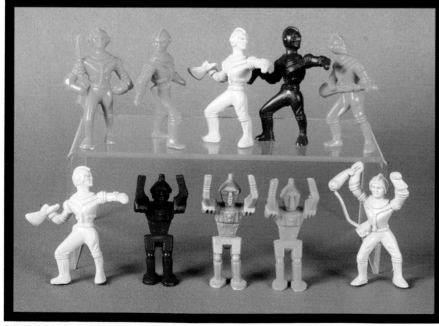

SET OF SPACEMEN, ROBOTS AND SPACEWOMAN
Circa 1952. Archer Plastics Inc.

SPACE PATROL ROCKET RING
1952. Ralston Purina Co.

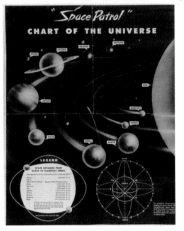

SPACE PATROL HANDBOOK AND CHART OF THE UNIVERSE
1952. Ralston Purina Co.

SPACE PATROL COSMIC CAP
Circa 1950s. Bailey of Hollywood.

SPACE PATROL LUNAR FLEET BASE PAPER MODEL KIT
1952. Ralston Purina Co.

THE WAR OF THE WORLDS PLAYSET
1953. Archer Plastics Inc.

CAPTAIN VIDEO FLYING SAUCER RING WITH INSTRUCTIONS
1951. Post Toasties.

CAPTAIN VIDEO DECODER
Circa 1950s. Unknown mfg.

Premiering in 1949, the Du-Mont network's *Captain Video* was first played by Richard Coogan and later Al Hodge, who also voiced Green Hornet for radio. From the opening, sing-song "Captain Vi-deeee-oh," kids spent five nights a week from 7-7:30 glued to their sets, watching the brave Captain and his Video Ranger (Don Hastings) fight space villains like the dastardly Dr. Pauli while preserving otherworldly justice in the year 2254. With devices such as the Opticon Scillometer and the Discatron (none of which actually did any real harm), Captain Video ushered in a glorious age of space adventuring heroes.

Despite the program's futuristic theme, it was notoriously low budget but innovative for its time. Even the name *Captain Video* itself was pioneering; "Captain" was already a common heroic title thanks to Captain America, Captain Marvel, and Captain Midnight, but the word "video" wasn't nearly as well-known.

As one of the most popular children's shows of its time, *Captain Video* produced plenty of toys, comics and even a Rangers Club. 1951-1952 even saw the debut of a 15-chapter movie serial starring Judd Holdren that drew kids in with an exciting new chapter in theaters every week.

In 1953, the TV series was dropped from five nights to just one night a week. In 1956, it was cancelled altogether, and Captain Video hung up his helmet for the last time.

1946 - 1960

139

Cowboys dominated children's television in the decade after World War II then did the same in primetime from 1955 to the early '60s. Following the 1920s successes of Tom Mix, Ken Maynard, William S. Hart, and Rin Tin Tin, many more six-gun heroes emerged in the '30s. The Lone Ranger debuted on radio in 1933, William Boyd first played Hopalong Cassidy in 1935, Gene Autry starred in his first serial that same year, and Roy Rogers (Leonard Slye) had his first starring role in 1938's *Under Western Skies*. These three men and the fictional Lone Ranger enjoyed fame and fortune in movies, radio, newspaper strips and comic books, and as pioneering TV cowboys.

Boyd capitalized first on the television medium with broadcasts of his old films. *The Hopalong Cassidy Show* went national on NBC in 1950, consistently ranking among the top three programs nationwide. Hundreds of Hoppy items flooded stores from bicycles to wallpaper to grape juice.

Also forging a trail on TV were *The Lone Ranger* (1949-1957), *The Cisco Kid* (1950-1956), *The Gene Autry Show* (1950-1956) and *The Roy Rogers Show* (1951-1957). Roy's merchandising empire followed on the same scale as Boyd's. Also successfully making the transition from radio to television were *Death Valley Days* (1952-1975) and *Sergeant Preston of the Yukon* (1955-1958), while *Straight Arrow* (1948-1951) was broadcast on radio only.

Davy Crockett's real-life adventures were fictionalized on the *Disneyland* television show in episodes airing from 1954 to 1956 starring Fess Parker. The show's theme, "The Ballad of Davy Crockett," shot to the top of the music charts and ten million coonskin hats were sold to young Crockett wanna-bes.

By the mid-1950s Americans' love of westerns was insatiable. Over thirty-five cowboy-themed shows debuted, seven in 1955 alone. Late '50s western programs aiming at a more adult audience included *Bonanza*, *The Life and Legend of Wyatt Earp*, *The Rifleman*, *Wagon Train*, *Maverick*, *Gunsmoke* and *Have Gun, Will Travel*.

HOPALONG CASSIDY OUTFIT
Circa 1950s. Various Mfgs.

ANNIE OAKLEY COWGIRL PLAYSUIT
Circa 1955. Anne Oakley Enterprise.

HOPALONG CASSIDY MASK PROTOTYPE
Circa 1950s. From the Sam and Gordon Gold archives.

LONE RANGER HEALTH AND SAFETY CLUB KIT
Circa 1954. Merita Bread.

STRAIGHT ARROW BANDANA SLIDE
1949. Nabisco.

STRAIGHT ARROW JIGSAW PUZZLES
1949. The Advertisers Service Div. Inc.

"Kaneewah, Fury!" Straight Arrow's cry to summon his horse resonated through the radio from 1948-1951. Steve Adams was owner of the Broken Bow Ranch, but he was also secretly an orphaned Comanche Indian raised by a white family. When Steve saw "justice, fair play and all good things" challenged, he would head to a secret cave and emerge as Straight Arrow in war paint and brilliant dress. No one knew his true identity except for his faithful side-kick Packy McCloud. With his golden palomino Fury (named via a contest that offered a real pony as a prize!), Straight Arrow protected the innocent and punished the guilty.

Howard Culver played the title character, while Fred Howard played Packy and Gwen Delano played housekeeper Mesquite Molly. The show featured the usual sharp-shooting western adventure but it also boasted one of the only Native American characters at the forefront of popular culture at that time.

Conceived to promote Nabisco's Shredded Wheat, Straight Arrow also turned up in a 1950-1952 newspaper strip, a 1950-1956 comic book, and premiums like a Mystic Wrist Kit, Indian war drum, feathered headband and arrowhead flashlight. Nabisco also printed a series of Injun-Unity cards found in boxes of Shredded Wheat. The cards offered information about Native American culture and were later reissued in bound volumes.

1946 - 1960

Many of America's favorite comic characters emerged from World War II ready to test their popularity beyond newspapers, comic books and radio. Superman was among the most successful with two movies in 1948 and 1950 starring Kirk Alyn and a third starring George Reeves in 1951. Reeves reprised his role on television in *The Adventures of Superman* from 1952-1958. Phyllis Coates was the original Lois Lane, followed by Noel Neill in 1953; Jack Larson played Jimmy Olsen.

Ralph Byrd starred as Dick Tracy in four feature films from 1945-1947. A live-action television show on ABC also starred Byrd in 1950-1951, but his death in 1952 ended the program. Captain Marvel, Batman, Captain America, Captain Midnight, Spy Smasher, and the Phantom also made the leap to film serials. Popeye cartoons were syndicated for television in 1956, and in 1956-1957, a Li'l Abner Broadway musical comedy enjoyed 700 performances.

The comic strip veterans of the late '40s welcomed new creations to the funny pages. Walt Kelly's *Pogo*, the wise possum of Okefenokee Swamp, with his eccentric supporting cast of critters was syndicated in 1951. *Beetle Bailey* began his tour of duty in 1950 and in 1951 Hank Ketcham introduced *Dennis the Menace* based on his own son's antics. In 1954, Bill Gaines adopted a 19th century cartoon icon as the trademark for his humor publication *MAD*, naming him Alfred E. Neuman–the freckle-faced kid known for his motto, "What, Me Worry?"

1950 saw the introduction of probably the most successful comic strip of all time–*Peanuts*. Charles Schulz originated the strip a few years earlier in the *St. Paul Pioneer Press* under the title *Li'l Folks* but it was renamed when syndicated by United Features. The life of unlikely hero Charlie Brown, his dog Snoopy, Linus, Lucy and friends inspired numerous reprint books, feature-length films, prime time television specials and a musical comedy.

DENNIS THE MENACE NAPKINS
Circa 1954. Monogram of California.

SET OF LITTLE LULU GLASSES
1951. Owen Illinois Glass Co.

PEANUTS DAILY STRIP ART
1953. Charles Schulz.

CAPTAIN MARVEL BANKS
Circa 1948. Fawcett Publishing

The contemplative pooch with the Walter Mitty lifestyle and a doghouse that seemed bigger on the inside (it even housed a Van Gogh!) first appeared in the *Peanuts* comic strip on October 4, 1950. At first he was just a cute stray dog who wasn't necessarily owned by Charlie Brown, but creator Charles Schulz humanized the mutt, let us into his thoughts and transformed him into the strip's most popular cast member and one of the world's most beloved childhood icons.

In his fantasy guises, Snoopy has battled the Red Baron as a WWI flying ace, cruised the college campuses as Joe Cool, dabbled in figure skating with Sonja Henie, and in what may be the nadir of his existence, donned leg warmers and headband to become "Flash Beagle."

Snoopy was born at the Daisy Hill Puppy Farm along with brothers Spike, Marbles, Andy and Olaf and sister Belle. His faithful friend Woodstock is a little yellow bird that is often at Snoopy's side; Snoopy even leapt into battle with the vicious cat next door when he thought the feline had captured Woodstock (it was just a glove).

Snoopy has appeared on every form of merchandise known to Man and has even traveled to the Moon, lending his name to Apollo 10's lunar module (the command module was dubbed 'Charlie Brown'). Through it all, he has remained a perfect blend of innocence and intellectualism. Good grief, he's the best.

SET OF PEANUTS FIGURES
1958. Hungerford.

1946 - 1960

REVOLUTION

The times they are a-changin'.
—*Bob Dylan*

America entered the 1960s with a sense of great expectations. President Kennedy galvanized a generation by telling them "Ask not what your country can do for you; ask what you can do for your country." African Americans challenged the status quo with demonstrations and a historic march on Washington.

The assassination of the President on November 22, 1963 shocked the entire nation, but President Lyndon B. Johnson's promise of a "Great Society" offered hope. Hope dimmed with the escalation of conflict in Vietnam. Tensions rose at home between races and generations. Civil rights leader Martin Luther King Jr. and presidential hopeful Robert F. Kennedy were assassinated in 1968 and America was embroiled in violence and despair. The '68 Democratic National Convention in Chicago erupted into a full-scale riot.

On the screen, James Bond was king, Julie Andrews' *The Sound of Music* broke box office records, and Man explored space and time in *2001: A Space Odyssey* and *Planet of the Apes*.

Four mop-top musicians from Liverpool came to the US, ushering in the British Invasion. A record company in Detroit gave us the Motown sound. In Southern California, things got psychedelic. And as an upbeat coda to a tumultuous time, the nation's youth celebrated with a Summer of Love and a three-day festival of "Peace and Music" at the Woodstock Music and Art Festival.

BATMAN NIGHT LIGHT
Circa 1966. Unknown Mfg.

THE BEATLES TOY GUITAR
Circa 1964. Selcol Products Ltd.

**SET OF THE MOTOWN
REVUE TICKETS**
1964. National Ticket Co.

HONEY WEST DOLL
1965. Gilbert.

149

Batman and Robin leapt onto the small screen in 1966 with a campy mix of big name guest star villains, gaudy costume and set design, and a delightfully tongue-in-cheek approach to superheroics that won over adults and children alike. For three seasons, and occasionally with the aid of Batgirl and the woefully inept police of Gotham City, the Dynamic Duo fought the forces of evil and virtually set the standard—for good or bad—by which we judged superheroes and comics for decades to come.

Batman had already undergone a 'new look' renovation in the pages of DC Comics, spearheaded by artist/editor Carmine Infantino, when producer William S. Dozier conceived of bringing the Caped Crusaders to television with a serial-style adventure series that would take nothing too seriously despite its earnest heroes and dastardly death traps. Adam West and Burt Ward played Batman and Robin alongside a veritable A-list of Hollywood stars eager to please their children or grandchildren and match wits with the crime-fighters. Cesar Romero (The Joker), Burgess Meredith (The Penguin), Frank Gorshin (The Riddler) and Julie Newmar (Catwoman) headlined a rotating rogues gallery that also featured Roddy McDowall, Vincent Price, Tallulah Bankhead and Joan Collins.

Batman even made it to the big screen in 1966 with a feature film version of the show that replaced Newmar with Lee Meriwether but retained all of the series' action and humor. "Some days you just can't get rid of a bomb" was just one of the lines West had to deliver with a straight face.

The merchandising of Batman and Robin kicked into overdrive and the psychedelic camp of the show would become inextricably linked with both Batman and American comic books in general. Today, newspaper stories heralding the latest events in comics invariably begin with the words that were once emblazoned on TV screens as Batman and Robin duked it out with their foes—"Bam! Pow! Zap!"

BATMAN CARD GAME
1966. Ideal Toy.

BATMAN BUTTON
1966. Button World Mfg. Co.

BATMAN AND ROBIN NAPKINS
1966. Amscan.

BATMAN AND ROBIN MUG
1966. Unknown Mfg.

BATMAN SHOOTING ARCADE
1966. Marx.

BATMAN NITE-LITE
1966. Snapit.

BATMAN PIX-A-GO-GO SCROLL VIEWER
1966. Embree Manufacturing Co.

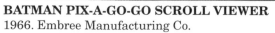

THE GREEN HORNET BLACK BEAUTY CAR
1966. Corgi Toy.

DAN & DALE BATMAN AND ROBIN LP
1966. Tifton Record Co.

When the Green Hornet and Kato appeared on the *Batman* TV show to help their caped friends battle Colonel Gumm, few viewers knew that the emerald adventurer had as rich a history as Batman himself, not to mention an equally famous relative.

Britt Reid, publisher of the *Daily Sentinel*, began his crime-fighting escapades on radio in 1936. The great-nephew of the Lone Ranger, Reid (originally voiced by Al Hodge) donned a mask, battered fedora and business suit to continue the family business as the Green Hornet.

Created by Lone Ranger visionary George W. Trendle and written mostly by Fran Striker, the Green Hornet had a cutting-edge weapon (a gun that shot non-lethal gas), a souped-up supervehicle (an ebony limousine nicknamed Black Beauty), a beautiful love interest who discovered his secret identity (the stunning Miss Case, who doubled as his secretary), and of course a trusty sidekick content to lurk in the shadows until needed (the first Japanese then Filipino valet, Kato).

Several actors took over for Hodge during the radio show's run, which lasted until 1952. The Green Hornet also turned up in movie serials and comic books. When *The Green Hornet* finally appeared for just one season on ABC television, Van Williams played the title role while martial arts guru Bruce Lee was Kato; both also turned up for the *Batman* guest appearance.

1961 - 1970

Folk music was the rage, led by chart toppers Peter, Paul and Mary, The Kingston Trio, Joan Baez and Bob Dylan. Pop music was getting an infusion of more intricate craftsmanship via Phil Spector's "Wall of Sound." Berry Gordy started a company in Detroit, dubbed it Hitsville, USA, and delivered that Motown sound with acts like the Miracles, The Temptations, Mary Wells, The Four Tops, The Four Seasons, Little Stevie Wonder and Marvin Gaye. Down in Memphis, Satellite Records changed its name to Stax and released records by Rufus Thomas, Booker T and the MGs, Sam and Dave, and Otis Redding. Elvis, fresh from the Army, conquered the charts with "Suspicion" and "Good Luck Charm" and filled movie theaters with *Blue Hawaii* and *Viva Las Vegas*.

In 1962, a popular Liverpool band released their first hit single in England, "Love Me Do." Less than two years later the entire world was conquered by the Beatles. Their names are as familiar today as they were in 1964–John, Paul, George and Ringo. Beatlemania led to the British invasion and soon the charts were filling up with England's newest hit makers–The Dave Clark Five, The Kinks, The Animals, Herman's Hermits, The Who and The Rolling Stones. Not to be outdone, American youth took to their guitars–The Byrds, Jimi Hendrix, Jefferson Airplane, The Grateful Dead and Janis Joplin. Even television joined in with the Monkees, an American group assembled to mimic the Beatles for a TV series. Despite their dubious beginnings, the group became one of the decade's biggest acts.

The culmination of '60s youth culture and music was the legendary Woodstock Music and Art Festival. Nearly 500,000 people gathered at Max Yasgur's dairy farm in Bethel, New York on August 15-17, 1969 to take in "3 Days of Peace & Music." The event distilled a generation's yearning spirit and was captured on film for a 1970 feature, *Woodstock*.

JET MAGAZINE VOL. 28 #12
1965. Johnson Publishing Co.

WOODSTOCK SOUNDTRACK LP
1970. Cotillion Records

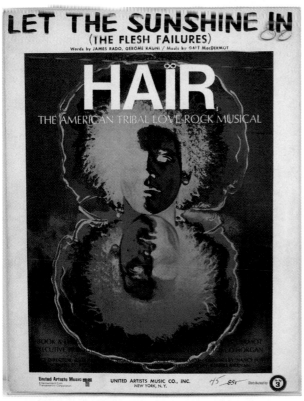

LET THE SUNSHINE IN (THE FLESH FAILURES) SHEET MUSIC
1968. United Artists Music Co.

SET OF BOB DYLAN CONCERT TICKETS
1966. National Ticket Co.

1961 - 1970

155

BOX SET OF THE BEATLES FIGURES
Circa 1964. Subbuteo Ltd.

**YELLOW SUBMARINE
AND HELP!
ONE-SHEETS**
1965-1968. United Artists.

**CAN YOU JERK LIKE ME AND WHERE
WERE YOU WHEN I NEEDED YOU
SHEET MUSIC**
1964-1966. Various Mfgs.

TWIST AROUND THE CLOCK LOBBY CARD
1961. Columbia Pictures.

THE MONKEES LUNCHBOX
1967. King-Seeley Thermos Co.

THE MONKEES BUTTON
1966. N.G. Slater.

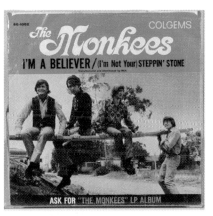

THE MONKEES I'M A BELIEVER/"I'M NOT YOUR" STEPPING STONE 45 SINGLE
1966. Colgems.

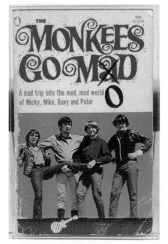

THE MONKEES GO MOD BOOK
1967. Popular Library.

SPOTLIGHT ON... THE MONKEES

The "Pre-Fab Four" were born when NBC decided to duplicate the pop culture punch of the Beatles with a stateside counterpart. Assembling a band from two actors (Mickey Dolenz, Davy Jones) and two musicians (Peter Tork, Michael Nesmith), the network debuted the fast-paced slapstick series *The Monkees* on September 12, 1966. Incorporating original songs in every episode, the band was soon very real and "comin' to your town" in numerous live tours.

The Monkees' success led to the inevitable merchandising bonanza, which included comic books, gum card sets, talking hand puppets, fan buttons, photo flip booklets and of course albums that included such hits as "Last Train to Clarksville," "I'm a Believer" and "Daydream Believer."

When the group demanded more creative control over their music, things began to change. The TV show ended after two years in 1968, but the band played on for several more albums, losing members Tork then Nesmith before calling it quits with the appropriately titled *Changes* in 1970. Along the way they also appeared in the critically revered piece of cinematic psychedlia, *Head*.

Years later, a new generation discovered the Monkees through an MTV revival of the show in 1985. The band reformed (minus Nesmith) for a 20th anniversary reunion and continued to tour off and on in various combinations for the next twenty years.

1961 - 1970

It may have blossomed with President John F. Kennedy in 1961, when he listed Ian Fleming's *From Russia With Love* as one of his favorite books. America was clamoring for the exploits of a new hero. Suave, sophisticated, and steel-eyed, this ladies' man who was licensed to kill leapt to the silver screen in *Dr. No* (1962) and captured moviegoers with his first line: "Bond. James Bond."

Audiences indulged in the exploits of this dapper espionage agent, code named 007, who traveled to exotic locales, romanced beautiful women, prevented evil men from taking over the world, and drank his vodka martinis "shaken, not stirred." Throughout the 1960s, the Bond films—produced by Albert R. Broccoli and Harry Saltzman—became undisputed box office champions. Sean Connery played the role with aplomb, becoming synonymous with the character and one of Hollywood's highest paid stars.

Bond's popularity carried over into a non-Broccoli/Saltzman production, the satirical *Casino Royale*, which featured seven James Bonds. Even replacing Connery with the untested George Lazenby in *On Her Majesty's Secret Service* didn't keep audiences away, resulting in what some fans regard as the best of Bond's cinematic adventures.

Secret agents were now all the rage. Cinemas saw Dean Martin, James Coburn and Michael Caine essay the roles of agents Matt Helm, Derek Flint and Harry Palmer. Television spies included Napoleon Solo and Illya Kuryakin in *The Man from U.N.C.L.E.*; April Dancer in *The Girl from U.N.C.L.E.*; John Steed and Emma Peel in *The Avengers*; *Honey West*; Simon Templar—future Bond Roger Moore—in *The Saint*; the IMF team of *Mission: Impossible*; Kelly Robinson and Alexander "Scotty" Scott in *I Spy*; *Modesty Blaise*; and Max and Agent 99 in the spy parody, *Get Smart!* Each week, audiences could watch their favorite heroes battle evil conglomerates like S.P.E.C.T.R.E., T.H.R.U.S.H., and KAOS.

JAMES BOND 007 SPY TRICKS
1965. Gilbert.

GET SMART LUNCHBOX
1966. King-Seely Thermos Co.

JOHN DRAKE SECRET AGENT GAME
1965. Milton Bradley.

**SECRET AGENT'S ASTON-MARTIN
BATTERY OPERATED CAR**
Circa 1960s. Japan.

THE MAN FROM U.N.C.L.E. GUM CARDS IN BOX
Circa 1965. Topps Chewing Gum Inc.

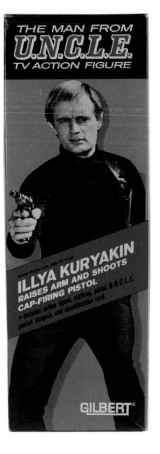

THE MAN FROM U.N.C.L.E. ILLYA KURYAKIN ACTION FIGURE
1965. Gilbert Co.

SPOTLIGHT ON...
THE MAN FROM U.N.C.L.E.

An admitted intentional television spoof of James Bond movies – Bond creator Ian Fleming even drafted the original outline for the series – *The Man From U.N.C.L.E.* was first telecast on NBC on September 22, 1964. For four seasons, the United Network Command for Law and Enforcement team battled the international crime syndicate known as THRUSH. U.N.C.L.E. was headed by Alexander Waverly (Leo G. Carroll), whose singular function was to hand out assignments and follow them up from the security of his secret office somewhere in New York City. His dour, dutiful agents were Napoleon Solo (Robert Vaughn) and Ilya Kuryakin (David McCallum).

Episodes were generally titled "The [title] Affair." Solo and Kuryakin defeated THRUSH through ingenuity, exotic weaponry and gadgets, and often with the aid of ordinary citizens. The hour-long show spawned a one season spin-off series in 1966, *The Girl From U.N.C.L.E.*, starring Stefanie Powers in the title role of April Dancer. Her efforts were also directed by the overworked Mr. Waverly.

The series ended in 1968, but various episodes were re-edited into eight feature films that did well in the US and Europe. A 1983 TV-movie reunion with Vaughn and McCallum, *The Return of the Man From U.N.C.L.E.*, even featured an amusing cameo by one-time James Bond, George Lazenby, as "J.B."

Comic book historians refer to the era from 1956 to 1970 as the Silver Age, when superheroes reasserted their dominance in American comic books. During this period, the DC heroes—Superman, Batman, Wonder Woman, The Flash, Green Lantern, Hawkman, The Atom—cemented their place in the annals of American pop culture. But in 1961, Marvel Comics introduced its own brand of superhero beginning with *Fantastic Four* #1, and soon the Marvel mix of accentuated humanity and far-flung fantasy made them the most popular comic books of the 1960s.

DC's Superman was still the front-runner in merchandising, with the Man of Steel featured on everything from puzzles to wallets; he was even the subject of a less than successful 1966 Broadway musical! Batman was enjoying a new surge in visibility thanks to a 1964 redesign in the comics and his 1966 television and feature film debut.

There weren't many items in the '60s featuring Marvel heroes like the Incredible Hulk, The Avengers, X-Men, Iron Man, Daredevil and the Amazing Spider-Man just yet, but Marvel did debut its first fan club in 1964, the Merry Marvel Marching Society. Instructing "True Believers" to "face front" and "be true to the Marvel Code of Ethics," the Society offered corny rhetoric and a few premiums, cleverly creating a self-motivated marketing force out of Marvel's own dedicated readers and making them feel like they were part of a cultural movement. The editorial voice crafted by Stan Lee for the comic book letters' pages and the club distinguished the more youthful, casual Marvel style from its "Distinguished Competition."

Marvel even encouraged its readers to catch mistakes in the comics themselves. Anyone who not only found an error in a Marvel comic but also explained it would receive a "No-Prize" in the mail. Dedicated Marvelites were thrilled to open their mailbox and find the fabled reward—an empty envelope with the words "No-Prize" emblazoned on the front. 'Nuff said.

WONDER WOMAN PUPPET
1966. Ideal Toy Co.

THE FLASH GAME
1967. Hasbro.

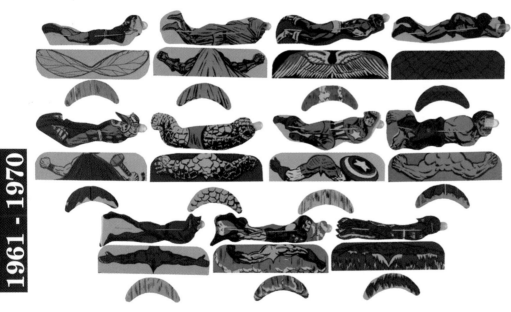

SET OF MARVEL FLYERS PACKAGE AND EXAMPLES
Circa 1966. Topps Chewing Gum.

AMAZING SPIDER-MAN #50
1968. Marvel Comics.

SPIDER-MAN PUPPET
1966. Ideal Toy Co.

SPIDER-MAN WIND-UP TRICYCLE
1968. Louis Marx & Co.

Stan Lee has told the story of Spider-Man's creation so many times that fans could recite it by rote. Suffice to say with the inestimable artistic contributions of Steve Ditko and Jack Kirby, Lee crafted a character with instant reader identification – a smart but socially ostracized high school student named Peter Parker whose life was changed forever when a radioactive spider bit his hand and imbued him with, dare we say it, "amazing" powers. But when his inaction led to the death of his Uncle Ben, Peter Parker learned that fancy powers weren't enough, for with "great power comes great responsibility." Spider-Man was born.

Spider-Man debuted in *Amazing Fantasy* #15 in 1962 and soon became one of the most ubiquitous heroes in the Marvel Comics universe, appearing in countless series of his own as well as a plethora of other titles. Spider-Man merchandise also proliferated; by the 1970s and '80s, the friendly neighborhood wall-crawler was represented in cartoons, live-action TV, books, magazines, records, video games, toys and household items of all kinds. Spidey may not often be popular in his own world, but in ours he was a smash hit.

The character got another pop culture boost with the release of his first-ever live-action feature film, *Spider-Man* (2002), starring Tobey Maguire. Today, there is more Spider-stuff in stores than you can shake a web at.

1961 - 1970

SET OF BARBIE DOLLS
1959-1960. Mattel.

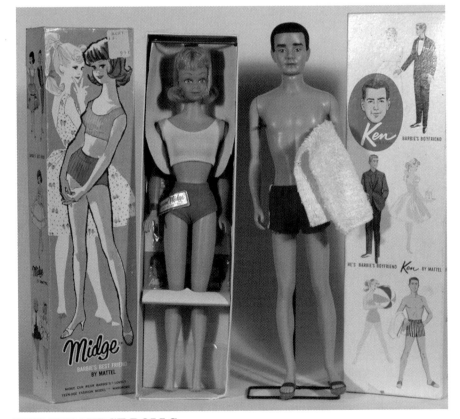

KEN AND MIDGE DOLLS
1961-1963. Mattel.

CAPTAIN ACTION ACTION FIGURE
1966. Ideal Toy Co.

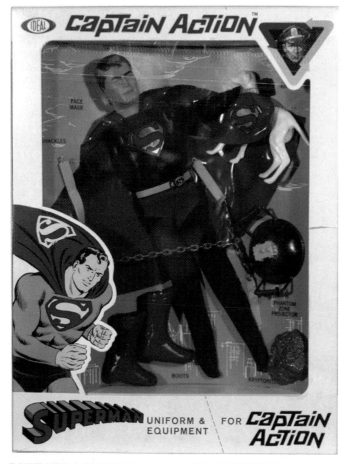

CAPTAIN ACTION SUPERMAN UNIFORM
1966. Ideal Toy Co.

Seeing the success of Barbie and GI Joe, Ideal Toys' Stan Wesson conceived a competitor and Captain Magic was born. By the time the world's first superhero action figure reached shelves, he had been renamed Captain Action.

The first Captain Action was 12" tall in a blue and black costume with the initials "CA" emblazoned on his chest. He also came with a dark blue captain's hat, black boots, belt, lightning sword, ray gun and fold-out mini poster. Later accessories included parachutes, mini-comics and video-matic flasher rings.

Sold separately were costumes that could transform Captain Action into the world's greatest superheroes: Superman, Batman, Aquaman, Captain America, the Phantom, Steve Canyon, Flash Gordon, Sgt. Fury and the Lone Ranger.

In 1967, sidekick Action Boy was introduced; he could take on the identities of Robin, Superboy or Aqualad. That same year, four more Captain Action costumes were released, each with rings for kids to wear: Green Hornet, Buck Rogers, Tonto and Spider-Man.

A later Action Boy dubbed "the bold adventurer" had a space-age motif, while 1968 unveiled nemesis Dr. Evil, a wretched creation with gigantic eye sockets and an exposed brain affectionately known as "the sinister invader of earth."

In addition to other toys and accessories, Captain Action also appeared in a five-issue comic book published by DC.

1961 - 1970

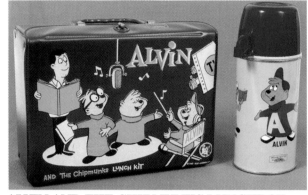

ALVIN AND THE CHIPMUNKS LUNCHBOX
1963. Thermos Co.

ALFRED E. NEUMAN BUST
1960. Contemporary Ceramics.

BABA LOOEY PUNCH-OUT BOOK
1961. Golden Press Inc.

HUCKLEBERRY HOUND CAR
1962. Marx.

SET OF FLINTSTONE DOLLS
Circa 1960s. Unknown Mfg.

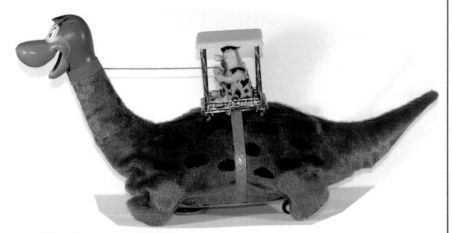

FLINTSTONES BATTERY OPERATED TOY
1962. Louis Marx & Co.

One of the longest-running prime time cartoons in TV history took place in prehistoric times. The Flintstones focused on a "modern stone age family," Fred and Wilma Flintstone, and their neighbors, Barney and Betty Rubble. The show was based on one of the most beloved programs of the 1950s, *The Honeymooners*.

The Hanna Barbera production aired for the first time on ABC on September 30, 1960. Audiences were introduced to the characters through intense advertising featuring Fred, Wilma and the gang in the weeks leading up to the show's premiere.

From the concrete-wheeled convertible that was powered by "the courtesy of Fred's two feet" to appliances that were actually animals, like Wilma's wooly mammoth dishwasher and Fred's bird-beak turntable, these stone age characters weren't in the dark about modern conveniences. During the show's six-year run, new and exciting things were always happening in the lives of the two families that went beyond their day-to-day shenanigans. 1962 saw the birth of Pebbles Flintstone, and later Barney and Betty got their own "bundle of noise" in the form of club-wielding, super-strong Bamm-Bamm. And who could forget the meddlesome alien, the Great Gazoo?

Today, shows like *The Simpsons* and *Family Guy* owe their success (and much of their format and design) to this paleolithic cartoon champ. "Yabba dabba doo!"

1961 - 1970

When President Kennedy committed America to putting a man on the moon by the end of the 1960s, all of the nation's resources were dedicated to making that dream come true. But before that journey became a reality, television producers were determined to take us on the ultimate trip where no one had gone before.

Producer Gene Roddenberry sold it to NBC as "*Wagon Train* to the stars," and when *Star Trek* debuted on September 8, 1966, it was just that–a western adventure series disguised as a journey into outer space, with a 23rd century maverick starship captain and his faithful crew forging new frontiers every week. Captain James T. Kirk (William Shatner), Spock (Leonard Nimoy) and Dr. McCoy (DeForest Kelley) headlined a cast that would become indelible icons in the annals of pop culture.

The western as a television genre was already long in the tooth by the 1960s, but there was still plenty of power left in those tales of dust and desperadoes–the long-running series *Gunsmoke* and *Bonanza*; the sci-fi western *The Wild, Wild West*; *The Big Valley*; and of course *Wagon Train*. It was *Star Trek*, however, that distilled the essence of the western while catapulting it into the distant future. Producer Irwin Allen countered with his own sci-fi/western hybrids like *Lost in Space* and *Voyage to the Bottom of the Sea*.

Long before it became a pop culture institution, *Star Trek* was just a moderately successful show that ran for three seasons and was almost always struggling to avoid cancellation. An unprecedented letter-writing campaign spearheaded by devoted fans actually saved the series for a third and final season, but eventually time ran out.

On July 21, 1969, Neil Armstrong and Buzz Aldrin of Apollo 11 became the first men to set foot on the surface of the moon. Less than two months later, the five-year mission of the U.S.S. Enterprise came prematurely to an end on September 2, 1969. But the adventure would continue...

THE ASTRONAUTS LUNCHBOX
Circa 1969. Aladdin Industries.

STAR TREK TRACER GUN REFILL DISCS
1966. Ray Plastic Inc.

STAR TREK ROCKET PISTOL
1967. Remco Industries.

1961 - 1970

MOON LANDING 3-D PLASTIC PICTURE
1969. Vari-Vue.

STAR TREK ENTERPRISE FRISBEE
1967. Remco Industries.

STAR TREK ASTRO-BUZZ RAY GUN
1967. Remco Industries.

THE LEGEND OF JESSE JAMES BOARD GAME
1966. Milton Bradley.

STAR TREK COLORING SET
1967. Hasbro.

STAR TREK BOARD GAME
1967. Ideal Toy Co.

With his greenish complexion, pointed ears, bowl haircut and upswept eyebrows, Leonard Nimoy's Mr. Spock – the half-Vulcan, half-human first officer of the USS Enterprise on TV's *Star Trek* – may not have seemed like a likely sex symbol, but almost as soon as the show debuted he became a magnet for female fans and the most recognizable character from the entire series.

The product of the union of an Earth woman with a Vulcan man, Spock struggled to reconcile his logical Vulcan side with his passionate human half. He was aided by his friendships with Captain James T. Kirk and Dr. McCoy, although McCoy's ribbing of Spock often sounded like anything but friendship.

The character also demonstrated Vulcan abilities like the nerve pinch and mind meld, making them permanent fixtures of pop culture.

Famously, early camera tests of Nimoy caused problems at the production office when the pictures kept coming back color-corrected by a lab that didn't realize Spock was supposed to look green!

Although Nimoy last appeared as Spock in 1991 on two episodes of *Star Trek: The Next Generation* and the film *Star Trek VI: The Undiscovered Country,* he remains one of the franchise's most enduring symbols. His struggle for identity and inner peace typified the 1960s in which he was born and continues to be relevant to audiences of every generation.

SET OF MARTIN LUTHER KING JR. FLICKER RINGS
Circa 1960s. Vari-Vue. Collection of Alex Winter.

CAPTAIN AMERICA #117
1969. Marvel Comics. First Falcon.

SPOTLIGHT ON...
THE FALCON

During this decade of change, comic book publishers moved to include more African-American heroes. Black Panther joined the Marvel universe and became a member of the Avengers. Other characters like DC's Black Lightning and Marvel's Black Goliath joined the ranks. Many of them had "black" in their name almost as if it was required.

First seen in *Captain America* #117, Sam Wilson was a street-savvy crime fighter known as the Falcon. He teamed up with Cap, and by #134 the series had a new title: *Captain America & The Falcon*. Much like the groundbreaking 1965 *I Spy* TV team of Robert Culp and Bill Cosby, Captain America and the Falcon was the first black and white duo in superhero comics.

They worked together for about 90 issues before going their separate ways. During that time, readers learned the true origin of the Falcon, saw him change costume, acquire his wings (a gift from Black Panther) and discover his mutant ability to communicate with his bird, Redwing.

Even after his departure, the team-ups with Cap didn't end. Falcon has also been an Avenger, once forced on the team as part of government regulations and later as an invited member. He starred in a solo story in *Marvel Premiere* and headlined his own miniseries. The Falcon still appears periodically in the pages of *Captain America*, helping to fight for his country regardless of race, creed or color.

1961 - 1970

For entertainment as well as the nation itself, it was a decade of change. Radio lost its edge, television went to color, movies became more daring, sports heroes became sports celebrities and advertisements were more memorable than the main feature.

Carrying over into the new decade, TV audiences took in the innocence of childhood with *Dennis the Menace* and *Leave it to Beaver*. Eliott Ness battled Al Capone weekly on *The Untouchables* and *The Ed Sullivan Show* entered the decade where it would have its most famous broadcast. The wit and wisdom of country folk was captured in *The Beverly Hillbillies*, *Green Acres*, and *Petticoat Junction*. Monsters, witches and aliens proved quite domestic in *The Addams Family*, *The Munsters*, *I Dream of Jeannie*, *Bewitched*, and *My Favorite Martian*. Stars had self-titled shows like *The Dick Van Dyke Show*, *The Andy Griffith Show*, *The Lucy Show*, *The Doris Day Show* and *The Dean Martin Show*. Batman got a friend with *The Green Hornet* and "Sock it to me" became a common expression thanks to *Rowan and Martin's Laugh-In*. Television also transformed sports players into international celebrities. Everyone knew Joe Namath, Willie Mays, Lew Alcindor, Sandy Koufax and Jack Nicklaus.

On the big screen, kids thrilled to *101 Dalmatians*, *Mary Poppins* and *The Love Bug*. Adults enjoyed *Charade*, *Breakfast at Tiffany's* and *Dr. Zhivago*. The emerging youth generation was reflected in *The Graduate*, *Easy Rider* and *Butch Cassidy and the Sundance Kid*. The past got bloody in *The Good, The Bad and the Ugly*, *The Wild Bunch* and *Bonnie and Clyde*. And everybody saw *The Sound of Music*.

With comic-style characters, infectious jingles and catchy slogans, memorable commercials convinced us to buy foods like Cheerios, Cap'n Crunch, Jif peanut butter, and Green Giant canned vegetables, as well as household items like Palmolive liquid, Ajax cleanser and Noxema Shaving Cream.

SELLING CELEBRITIES

JULIA LUNCHBOX
1969. King-Seeley Thermos Co.

SOUPY SALES DOLL
1965. Sunshine Doll Co.

MORTICIA ADDAMS HAND PUPPET
1964. Unknown Mfg.

THAT GIRL PAPER DOLL BOOK
1967. Saalfield.

I DREAM OF JEANNIE BOARD GAME
1965. Milton Bradley.

BEWITCHED #8
1967. Dell Publishing.

Inevitably, conversations about '60s sitcoms come down to the question, "Who's your favorite – Samantha (Elizabeth Montgomery) or Jeannie (Barbara Eden)?" The characters' differences and similarities are what make them so significant to viewers as each played her part in revolutionizing the way women's roles were perceived.

Bewitched debuted a year before *I Dream of Jeannie* as part of ABC's 1964 lineup. A fantasy sitcom about a witch's suburban life as the wife of a mortal, it was an instant hit, finishing its first season as the highest rated new series and spending its first five seasons in Nielsen's top twelve.

I Dream of Jeannie debuted on NBC in 1965, but some viewers considered Jeannie's subservient interaction with Tony "Master" Nelson (Larry Hagman) a step back from Samantha's progressive tactics in outwitting her husband, Darrin (Dick York, later Dick Sargent). Jeannie evolved during the show's five-year-run, however, and by the time the series ended in 1970 with Jeannie and Tony married, audiences realized that Jeannie, like Samantha, had a consistent history of achieving her own ends in her romantic and household dealings.

So whether women of the '60s asserted power overtly or feigned subservience to gain the upper hand, all seemed to find one or the other relatable. Family sitcoms have been following these marital archetypes ever since.

1961 - 1970

EXPANDING UNIVERSE

The Force will be with you...always.
—Obi-Wan Kenobi (Sir Alec Guinness), Star Wars

It was a period of unrest for the nation—political scandals from Watergate to Iran-Contra, increased urban crime and poverty, an energy crisis that left Americans waiting in line for hours to fill up their gas tanks, economic recession, and the continuing struggle for equality between the races and sexes. The '70s and '80s witnessed the end of Vietnam and the Cold War as well as the transition from an industrial to an information economy. As Americans turned inward during the "Me Decade" and the Reagan years, music became introspective with singer-songwriters while disco added glitz and glamour. Television offered equal parts social commentary and pure escapism. But the ultimate escape arrived in movie theaters, and its name was *Star Wars*.

A new era of high-tech entertainment transformed our daily lives. Americans gained access to communications, appliances, media recording devices and home entertainment centers that sped up the pace of life while connecting them with a world of entertainment, from personal computers and video games to video tape recorders (VCRs) and compact discs (CDs).

For children, this naturally meant even more sophisticated toys. Electronics allowed manufacturers to create a whole new category of playthings that could respond in innovative ways and interact with a child. In the '70s and '80s, childhood was defined by Saturday morning cartoons, primetime television, video arcades, plenty of breakfast cereal, and lots of toys.

THE FALCON DOLL
1974. Mego.

RETURN TO MORGAN'S ISLAND OIL PAINTING
1985. Carl Barks.

TONI TENNILLE DOLL
1977. Mego.

HAN SOLO ACTION FIGURE
1978. Kenner.

187

Although *Jaws* introduced Hollywood, America and the world to the idea of the summer blockbuster film release in the summer of 1975, it was George Lucas' *Star Wars*–a perfect blend of WWII-era serial adventure and cutting edge film-making technology–that cemented the notion of the blockbuster and transformed pop culture in one historic space-faring assault on movie goers.

It was May 25, 1977, and long before fans could have dreamed of such things as prequels, it wasn't even a trilogy. *Star Wars* was just one amazing film that captured the public's imagination and took them on an adrenaline-fueled ride through hyperspace. The movie introduced us to a lightsaber-wielding hero, a rogue with a heart of gold, a damsel in distress, two comical robot sidekicks, and a black hat (literally) villain with a pronounced breathing problem.

The overwhelming success of *Star Wars*–almost $776 million worldwide in box office returns to date–led to the production of two sequels–*The Empire Strikes Back*, released in 1980, and *Return of the Jedi*, released in 1983. Between 1977 and 1985, *Star Wars*-related merchandise in every category imaginable flooded store shelves, from toys based on the characters, vehicles and environments seen in the films to household items, clothing, and much more. The marketing juggernaut that was the *Star Wars* trilogy established a modern template for the exploitation of entertainment that continues to be followed to this day.

By the mid-'80s, with no new *Star Wars* movies on the horizon–except for a few forays into television with two live-action films starring the teddy bear-like Ewoks from *Return* and two short-lived animated series, *Droids* and *Ewoks*–the demand for all things *Star Wars* began to wane. But for an entire generation, three years was simply the wait between *Star Wars* movies.

Today, *Star Wars* is a permanent fixture in the American pop culture landscape. The Force will be with us...always.

LUKE SKYWALKER ACTION FIGURE
1978. Kenner.

SET OF JAWA AND POWER DROID ACTION FIGURES
1978-1979. Kenner.

1971 - 1990

SET OF BOBA FETT, LANDO CALRISSIAN AND YODA ACTION FIGURES
1980. Kenner.

THE EMPIRE STRIKES BACK REBEL ARMORED SNOW SPEEDER
1980. Kenner.

THE EMPIRE STRIKES BACK RE-RELEASE ONE-SHEET
1981. Twentieth Century Fox.

STAR WARS X-WING FIGHTER
Circa 1978. Kenner.

THE SAGA CONTINUES.

STAR WARS

REVENGE OF THE JEDI

Coming May 25, 1983 to your galaxy.

REVENGE OF THE JEDI ONE-SHEET
1983. Twentieth Century Fox. The title of the movie was changed prior to release, but some posters were already made.

EMPIRE STRIKES BACK SCOUT WALKER
1982. Kenner.

STAR WARS™
THE POWER OF THE FORCE

SPECIAL COLLECTORS COIN

Kenner

Romba

ROMBA ACTION FIGURE
1984. Kenner.

With his jet black cape and armor, robotic chest unit, burning red lightsaber, rasping breath, and fearsome mask and helmet inspired by ancient samurai (and possibly *The Fantastic Four*'s Doctor Doom), Darth Vader stepped from the mist in the opening moments of the first *Star Wars* movie in 1977 and instantly embodied pure evil for an entire generation. In a film filled with memorable images and stunning effects, Vader's visage was burned into the brain of fans and plastered on a plethora of items from toys and models to bedspreads and cereal boxes.

While just one Imperial threat to the Rebellion in *Star Wars* and apparently suborddinate to the cold, calculating Grand Moff Tarkin (Peter Cushing), Vader quickly became the series' main villain with the shocking revelation in 1981's *The Empire Strikes Back* that he was in fact the father of hero Luke Skywalker. The scene remains one of the most talked-about moments in movie history. By the third and final film in the trilogy, 1983's *Return of the Jedi*, Vader had redeemed himself by saving his son from the wrath of the Emperor, sacrificing his own life in the process.

Today, the character's backstory has been explored in detail via three 'prequel' *Star Wars* films, but throughout the 1980s, he was simply the ultimate bad guy, the worst father you could imagine, and the very embodiment of the Dark Side of the Force.

1971 - 1990

The genesis of home video and computer games actually goes back to the 1950s, when Ralph Baer conceived of using television sets to play games and William Higginbotham invented *Tennis for Two*, a precursor to *PONG*. The simple game with the bouncing ball and two lines for paddles officially debuted in 1972 and was an instant pop culture smash, appearing on *Saturday Night Live* and invading bars, arcades and homes in multiple incarnations since Higginbotham had never secured any ownership rights for the original game. Several companies released their own versions and variants of *PONG*, and home video game console systems quickly became Christmas shopping staples.

The first home systems included the Magnavox Odyssey (1972) and the Coleco Telstar (1976), but the quintessential console was the Atari 2600 (1977). Its faux wood-trimmed design, iconic joystick controllers and vast library of cartridge-based games defined the very concept of the home video game console, and with the debut of its first licensed game, *Space Invaders*, success was assured. Atari later offered the 5200 (1982) and 7800 (1986), but neither would match the impact of the 2600.

The early systems were soon joined by the Intellivision (1980), Colecovision (1982) and Vectrex (1982). The market was soon glutted, causing a backlash that subsided when the Nintendo Entertainment System arrived in 1985. Anchored by characters like Super Mario, Nintendo ushered in a new era for home video gaming that has yet to end.

By the end of the 1980s, video games were entering a new period of technological and cultural maturity with the release of the Nintendo Game Boy and the Sega Genesis system, both in 1989. The years ahead would lead to even more innovation—and controversy—but by the end of the '80s, video games had taken their place as an intrinsic and indelible part of American childhood, with characters like Pac-Man, Donkey Kong and Sonic the Hedgehog permanently joining the pop culture lexicon.

SET OF DONKEY KONG BANKS
1981-1982. Various Mfgs.

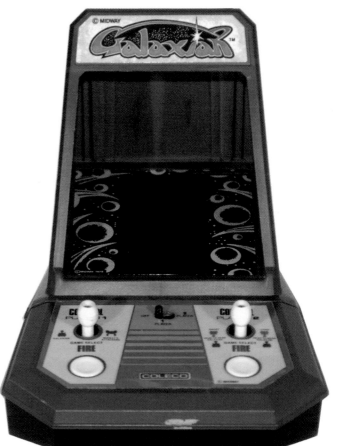

**SET OF DRACULA, BASEBALL AND
GALAXIAN VIDEO GAMES**
Circa 1980s. Various Mfgs.

SET OF PAC-MAN WIND-UP FIGURES
1982. Tomy.

SET OF PAC-MAN PUPPETS
Circa 1980s. Commonwealth.

Originally called *Puck Man* in Japan, the Namco game character that came to symbolize the explosion in video game popularity throughout the 1980s gained his current moniker when he made his US debut in 1980 through distributor Midway. Shortly thereafter, "Pac-Mania" ensued as the non-violent maze game enthralled young and old and infiltrated every aspect of popular culture. *Pac-Man* even trumped the previous most popular video game, *Space Invaders*, and left the little marching aliens in the dust.

One of the game's charms was that it was considered among the first to offer players the chance to adopt the persona of the game's "hero." About 290,000 *Pac-Man* arcade machines were sold between 1980 and 1987. Other video game manufacturers aped the *Pac-Man* formula of light-hearted adventure and puzzle-like play, introducing titles like *Q*Bert, Frogger* and *Donkey Kong*. Less scrupulous companies just ripped off the original, resulting in countless bootlegged versions.

Pac-Man's popularity led to spin-offs *Ms. Pac-Man, Super Pac-Man, Baby Pac-Man, Jr. Pac-Man* and *Pac-Land* among others. The character also turned up in cartoons, board games and a cascade of other merchandise that still continues to this day. In 1982, a song titled "Pac-Man Fever" hit the radio waves and demonstrated just how quickly and powerfully the little yellow glutton had won over the world.

When *Ms.* Magazine was launched by feminist Gloria Steinem in December 1971 with a special test issue inserted in copies of *New York Magazine*, turning "a movement into a magazine"—a quote attributed to *Ms.* founding editor Letty Cottin Pegrebin—the cover image may have seemed an odd choice. Striding colossus-like down a street under the banner "Wonder Woman for President," the Amazon Princess created by William Moulton Marston for DC Comics back in the '40s had been selected by the magazine as a shining example of American feminine power and independence, albeit in a skimpy costume.

Appearing on *Ms.* exactly thirty years after her debut in the pages of *All-Star Comics* #8, Wonder Woman's stint as cover model was nothing less than a rebirth for the star-spangled heroine, sparking the return of her classic costume in her own comic—she had recently taken to wearing a white pantsuit instead of her traditional attire—and setting her on the path to worldwide fame.

Just a few years later, Wonder Woman leapt into action for a television series in which Linda Carter embodied the beautiful and courageous heroine through three seasons of adventures on two different networks (ABC and CBS), establishing the character as a mainstream pop culture icon as never before and inspiring other strong female figures to step forward and make themselves heard. This unique mix of feminine assertiveness and sexuality coupled with the cheesy entertainment values of the '70s and '80s led to an entire wave of female-driven action and fantasy series, from *Charlie's Angels* and *Isis* to *Police Woman* and *Cagney & Lacey*.

By the time Sigourney Weaver battled a monster in *Alien* (1979) and *Aliens* (1986) and Linda Hamilton tousled with the T-800 in *Terminator* (1984) and *Terminator 2: Judgment Day* (1991), there was no doubt that brains, brawn and beauty were an unbeatable combination for any pop culture icon.

THE KROFFT SUPERSHOW LUNCHBOX
1976. Aladdin.

MISS PIGGY PAPER DOLL
1980. Colorforms.

SPACE: 1999 LUNCHBOX
1975. Thermos King-Seeley.

1971 - 1990

CHARLIE'S ANGELS VAN MODEL KIT
1977. Revell.

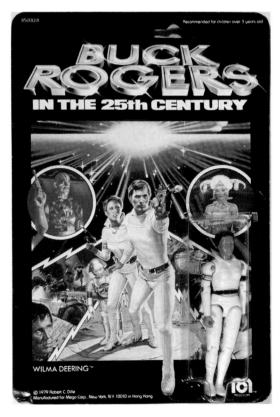

WILMA DEERING ACTION FIGURE
1979. Mego.

FLOJO DOLL
1989. LJN.

THE BIONIC WOMAN DOLL
1974. Kenner.

SET OF TEELA AND EVIL-LYN ACTION FIGURES
1982-1983. Mattel.

The fantasy action adventure TV series *The Six Million Dollar Man* starring Lee Majors as test pilot-turned-bionic secret agent Steve Austin was already a smash hit when a spin-off was conceived centering on a female counterpart to Austin. Jamie Sommers (Lindsay Wagner) was a tennis player and girlfriend of Steve's who appeared in several episodes before suffering an accident, receiving a familiar bionic upgrade and losing her memory of her love for Austin.

Sommers was then the subject of her own series, *The Bionic Woman*, which ran on ABC and then NBC from 1976-1978. Working undercover as a schoolteacher in Ojai, California, Sommers went on a variety of adventures that pitted her against the same mix of foreign agents, criminals, and occasional super-baddies that Austin faced in his own show. Sommers lived in a farmhouse she rented from Austin's mother; she even adopted a bionic dog named Maximillion (guess how much it cost to upgrade him). While the show was never as popular as the original series, it nevertheless helped to establish the characters as quintessential icons of '70s pop culture.

The bionic dynasty spawned a whole line of popular Kenner toys as well as books, comics and other merchandise. Three TV-movie reunions aired in 1987, 1989, 1994 at last brought Steve and Jamie back together, leading to a bionic marriage in the final film.

1971 - 1990

In the 1970s and '80s, American children woke up every Saturday morning to a treasure trove of entertainment, education and clever marketing, and then did it all again every day after coming home from school. The Saturday morning line-up, long a fixture of network television, experienced its last powerful period of influence on a generation of kids not yet introduced to cable TV and—much later—the Internet, as did the power-packed hours of programming that greeted them on local television stations just before dinner.

TV featured *Schoolhouse Rock*, Sid and Marty Krofft productions like *Land of the Lost*, *Electra Woman and Dyna Girl* and *Dr. Shrinker*, action adventure cartoons like *Thundercats* and *He-Man and the Masters of the Universe*—the first animated children's program specifically built around a toy line, light-hearted fare like *The Smurfs*, *Jem*, and *Rainbow Brite*, and an influx of Asian animé like *Robotech*, *Star Blazers* and *Voltron*. All the old theatrical cartoon shorts starring the likes of Bugs Bunny and Woody Woodpecker were repackaged into syndicated TV series, and an onslaught of food and toy commercials targeted kids when they were most likely to pay attention.

In the newspapers, venerable comic strips like *Peanuts*, *Dick Tracy* and *Dennis the Menace* were joined by *Doonesbury*, *Garfield*, *The Far Side*, *Bloom County*, and *Calvin & Hobbes*.

DC heroes Superman and Batman launched feature film franchises in 1978 and 1989 respectively that defined those characters in the minds of Americans for years to come and led to multiple sequels. Marvel superheroes found a home on the small screen with cartoons and live-action series devoted to *The Incredible Hulk* and *The Amazing Spider-Man*; both also made the leap to newspaper strips. *The Teenage Mutant Ninja Turtles* debuted in comics and then appeared in a cartoon series and a live-action feature film.

SPIDER-MAN AND THE HULK TOLIET PAPER
1979. Oh Dawn!

SET OF PEANUTS GLASSES
Circa 1980s. Unknown Mfg.

MARVEL COMICS SUPER HEROES LUNCHBOX
1976. Aladdin.

1971 - 1990

SET OF SNOOPY & BELLE DOLLS
Circa 1980s. Knickerbocker.

SPIDER-MAN COSTUME
Circa 1970s. Ben Cooper.

GARFIELD DOLL
1981 Dakin.

FAKER ACTION FIGURE
1983. Mattel.

TEENAGE MUTANT NINJA TURTLE MICHAELANGELO
1990. Mirage Studios.

203

Created by cartoonist Jim Davis, the newspaper comic strip *Garfield* debuted on June 19, 1978 and was a satire of the life of pet owners in which the true masters of the home are the pets. The master of loser Jon Arbuckle is undoubtedly his rotund orange cat Garfield, originally depicted as small-eyed and especially large. By 1984, Garfield began to look more like he does to this day, with larger eyes and a (slightly) slimmer waist.

Born in the kitchen of Mama Leone's Italian Restaurant to a stray cat named Sonja, Garfield developed a taste for lasagna in the short time he spent with his mother. Ever since then, it has always been his favorite food. Other than food, Garfield bases his life around sleeping and torturing the dim-witted but lovable dog Odie. Garfield hates Mondays and considers himself to be far more intelligent than anyone else around him.

As of 2006, *Garfield* was syndicated in roughly 2,570 newspapers and journals around the world and held the Guinness World Record for most widely syndicated comic strip. Davis still writes the strips while the illustrators at Paws, Inc. (Davis' company) produce all of the art. Garfield's popularity also led to an animated TV series and several specials, two feature-length live-action films, and millions of dollars in merchandising like the stuffed Garfields suction-cupped on car windows that were everywhere in the 1980s.

The "Happy Meal" is synonymous with fast food premium toys, all thanks to Dick Brams, a St. Louis regional advertising manager for McDonald's who spearheaded the meal-in-a-box program for children. It tested regionally in 1977-78 and then went national in 1979 with the debut of six Circus Wagon-themed boxes. Happy Meals then went to warp speed with the debut of their first movie tie-in that same year for *Star Trek: The Motion Picture*.

Costing just one dollar when they first appeared, Happy Meals went worldwide in the 1980s and competing chains rushed to keep up. Over the years, Burger King, Wendy's, Taco Bell, and many others have offered their own version of Happy Meals and premium toys.

Some food-related premiums, however, were as close as the kitchen table, hidden under all those Cheerios or Rice Krispies in the form of breakfast cereal premiums. With the advent of mass production of cheap plastic items and better packaging options, toys inside cereal boxes were everywhere, just another part of a balanced breakfast.

Food promotions were an intrinsic part of every blockbuster film released by the end of the '80s, with *Star Wars*, *E.T.*, *Ghostbusters*, and many others joining burgers, fries and cereal inside colorfully illustrated cardboard boxes. As in years past, toys also immortalized restaurant and cereal characters themselves, with Ronald McDonald, Grimace, Snap, Crackle and Pop, Toucan Sam, Tony the Tiger, and more turning up in toy form.

Today, thanks to Happy Meals, McDonald's is the largest toy distributor in the world, with between 3,000-5,000 toys offered over the last 25 years in the US alone, perhaps as many as 20,000 toys worldwide. Today, kids still rush with mom and dad to their local fast food restaurant or supermarket, hoping to "Collect 'em all!"

YOU WANT TOYS WITH THAT?

THE McDONALD'S GAME
1975. Milton Bradley.

OSCAR MAYER WEINERMOBILE
Circa 1980s. Oscar Mayer.

BURGER KING PILLOW
Circa 1970s. Burger King.

1971 - 1990

SET OF NABISCO COOKIE THEMED DOLLS
1983. Talbot Toys.

THE MAGICAL BURGER KING DOLL
1980. Knickerbocker.

SET OF DC SUPER HEROES COOKIES
1982. Nabisco.

206

RONALD McDONALD DOLL
1978. Hasbro.

The smiling clown pitchman from McDonaldland was a ubiquitous presence on television in the '70s and '80s, but his now-famous rhyming name almost didn't make the advertising cut.

Promotion agency Kal-Elrlich and Merrick initially planned to name McDonald's mascot "Archie McDonald" in recognition of the restaurant's golden arches. But when they found that there was already a personality named Arch McDonald in the DC area, they went back to the drawing board. Meteorologist Willard Scott eventually came up with the catchy new name and is also credited as the first man ever to don the yellow, red and white jump suit for several TV commercials in 1963.

Ronald's original look was designed by costumer Janet Vaughn. His hat was a tray with a styrofoam burger, bag of fries and a milkshake, his shoes were shaped like hamburger buns and his nose was an actual McDonald's cup. He also possessed the ability to pull whole hamburgers from his belt. We suspect sanity prevailed eventually, allowing Ronald to settle into a more familiar clown motif.

In 1971, Ronald was joined by a horde of characters that populated the magical world of McDonaldland, including Grimace (originally Evil Grimace), the Hamburglar, and the Fry Kids. McDonaldland was benevolently administered by Mayor McCheese, whose voice was based on Ed Wynn's lilting tones.

T he 1970s saw G.I. Joe join an Adventure Team that focused on environmental rather than military missions. With more realistic hair and "Kung Fu Grip," Joe was bigger than ever, but the resurgence was short-lived. Joe ended the first phase of his career battling global catastrophes in 1976. An 8-inch Super Joe line in 1977-78 failed to reignite interest. The impact of the energy crisis on the price of plastic spelled temporary retirement for Joe.

When G.I. Joe was recalled to active duty in 1982, he had lost some of his physical stature but none of his pop culture power. The new 3-3/4" size for action figures had been set by the success of Kenner's *Star Wars* toys, so Hasbro adopted that standard for the more articulated Joes. Now a team of individually named heroes with an enemy organization called Cobra, hundreds of accessories, vehicles and play sets, G.I. Joe was one of the ubiquitous toy lines of the 1980s, easily overshadowing its predecessor as *Star Wars* waned in popularity. In 1985, *Toy and Hobby World* ranked Joe as America's best-selling toy.

Joe's revival owed its success to a unique marketing partnership with a monthly Marvel comic book, an animated series, and a TV campaign that included the first commercial devoted to a comic book. While the comic and cartoon featured unrelated storylines, both developed the Joes into identifiable personalities, creating a cohesive world in which kids could play.

In the late '80s the line became more fantasy-oriented, with characters like Cobra leader Serpentor–featured in 1987's *G.I. Joe: The Movie*, subsets like the Iron Grenadiers and Battle Force 2000, and Joes modeled on real people like wrestler Sgt. Slaughter and football player William "The Refrigerator" Perry.

1989 marked Joe's 25th anniversary. By 1991, with the 3-3/4" line finally dwindling in popularity, the original 12" Joe returned in a Hall of Fame series. Today, G.I. Joe still battles for justice in all sizes. Kids know that G.I. Joe will always be a Real American Hero...and knowing is half the battle.

**G.I. JOE COBRA COMMANDER
ACTION FIGURE**
1985. Hasbro.

**G.I. JOE BARONESS
ACTION FIGURE**
1985. Hasbro.

SUPER JOE ADVENTURE TEAM FIGURE
1977. Hasbro.

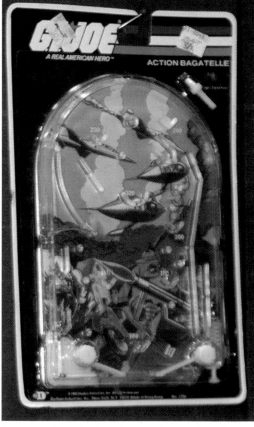

G.I. JOE ACTION BAGATELLE GAME
Circa 1980s. Hasbro.

G.I. JOE ZARTAN ACTION FIGURE
1986. Hasbro.

**G.I. JOE SNAKE EYES
ACTION FIGURE**
1985, Hasbro.

**G.I. JOE STORM SHADOW
ACTION FIGURE**
1985. Hasbro.

Arguably the most popular characters of the G.I. Joe universe, Snake-Eyes and Storm Shadow have an enormous fan following that has grown for over two decades. One-time friends and "Sword Brothers" from the same Ninja Clan, Snake-Eyes and Storm Shadow are now bitter enemies as Snake-Eyes battles alongside the heroes of G.I. Joe and Storm Shadow serves his terrorist masters in COBRA.

From their first appearances in Marvel Comics' *G.I. Joe* #1 (1982) and #21 (1984) respectively, both Snake-Eyes and Storm Shadow have been shrouded in mystery and intrigue, with the truth about their training, how they came to be with their organizations and even their identities remaining secret for years.

Snake Eyes and Storm Shadow served together during the Vietnam War and became so close that Storm Shadow offered Snake-Eyes a position in the "family business." After returning to the US to find his family dead, Snake-Eyes accepted the offer and began to train with Hard Master and Soft Master, uncles of Storm Shadow.

After three years of training, tragedy struck when Hard Master was killed by an assassin and a rift formed between the two friends. Snake-Eyes retreated to the High Sierras and Storm Shadow sought revenge for the death of his uncle and master. They met again years later but now on different sides of the never-ending battle for freedom.

1971 - 1990

Children in the '70s and '80s were as likely to grow up on a diet of old movies and television reruns as they were on new shows and films. TV syndication, the birth of cable and home video made all eras of entertainment available simultaneously.

The '70s saw experimentation in progressive rock via Genesis, Yes and Pink Floyd, and punk rock through the Ramones and the Clash. Swedish quartet ABBA scored with dance hall favorites like "Waterloo." Disco was popularized by the Bee Gees and the Village People, but gave way to New Wave bands like Blondie and Devo by the early '80s. The debut of MTV brought music videos by Madonna and Michael Jackson to the forefront. The song "We Are the World" united musicians in an effort to fight famine.

The '70s saw the birth of the blockbuster with *The Godfather*, *The Exorcist*, and *Jaws*. Disaster epics like *Airport*, *The Poseidon Adventure*, and *Earthquake* drew crowds. *Saturday Night Fever* brought disco to the movies, while *Grease* and *Animal House* offered nostalgic trips to the '50s and '60s. Aliens were friendly—*E.T.*, *Close Encounters of the Third Kind*—or deadly—*Alien*, *The Terminator*. *The Planet of the Apes* films (which began in 1968) spawned two TV series. Roger Moore stepped into the role of James Bond. *Star Wars'* Han Solo, Harrison Ford, traded his vest and blaster for a fedora and whip as Indiana Jones in *Raiders of the Lost Ark* and two sequels. And the original *Star Trek* cast returned in films that led to the debut of a TV sequel, *Star Trek: The Next Generation*.

Also on television, social boundaries were shattered on *All In the Family*, comedies like *Cheers* and *The Cosby Show* garnered huge ratings, and variety series *The Carol Burnett Show*, *The Flip Wilson Show*, *The Sonny & Cher Show* and *Donny and Marie* kept people smiling. *The Six Million Dollar Man* and *The Bionic Woman* offered sci-fi adventure, while those Duke boys kept getting into trouble on *The Dukes of Hazzard*.

ALIEN MODEL KIT
1979. MPC.

V ENEMY VISITOR DOLL
1984. LJN.

THE DUKES OF HAZZARD GENERAL LEE CAR
1981. Ertl.

1971 - 1990

213

**BATTLESTAR GALACTICA
COLONIAL WARRIOR**
1978. Mattel.

GREMLINS STRIPE DOLL
1984. LJN.

**GREMLINS GIZMO LOVES
YOU! PUZZLE**
1983. Hallmark.

**A CHRISTMAS STORY RED RYDER
BB GUN DISPLAY SIGN**
1984. Daisy.

**GHOSTBUSTERS DANCING
SLIMER RADIO**
1988. Justin Products Inc.

No. 46000   AGES 4 and up

INDIANA JONES ™

ACTION FIGURE

Indiana Jones, the daring archeologist and world adventurer of the movie, *Raiders of the Lost Ark*

STARRING IN

RAIDERS *of the* **LOST ARK** ™

Contents: Authentically styled 12" Action Figure with removable hat, jacket, shirt, pants, boots, holster, gun and whip.

Kenner Meets or exceeds all safety requirements of Product Standard 72-76

Indiana Jones

INDIANA JONES ACTION FIGURE
1981. Kenner.

If the combination of block-buster movie special effects and old-fashioned adventure had a name, it must be Indiana Jones. The fedora-wearing, bullwhip-wielding archaeologist was born in the minds of George Lucas and Steven Spielberg, appearing in three films from 1981-1989 and typifying the blend of gee-whiz '80s movie magic and '30s Republic serial thrills.

At first Tom Selleck, TV's *Magnum P.I.,* was set to play the part but his television schedule prevented it. Harrison Ford wound up playing Indy in *Raiders of the Lost Ark* (1981)*, Indiana Jones and the Temple of Doom* (1984) and *Indiana Jones and the Last Crusade* (1989). He also turned up for a cameo on a 1993 episode of Lucas' *The Young Indiana Jones Chronicles* TV series. Ford's Jones blended the suave arrogance of James Bond, the brash heroism of his own Han Solo from *Star Wars* and the adventurous style of Allan Quatermain. In the third film, Ford was even joined by the original film Bond himself, Sean Connery, as Indiana Jones' professor father.

Combining religious iconography – Indy was always after another mystical ancient relic with the Nazis or other foes hot on his heels – with comic book storytelling and action movie pacing, the Indiana Jones films grossed about 1.2 billion dollars worldwide and established the silhouette of Indiana Jones as one of the most recognizable heroes of any era.

215

Comic books have always had close ties to other media, but in the 1970s and '80s, the number of comic book adaptations of movie, TV and toy properties exploded, combining the medium's power to promote and sell an idea or a product with some of the most popular entertainment icons of the time.

The explosion began in 1977 with Marvel Comics' adaptation of *Star Wars*. Scripted by Archie Goodwin and illustrated by Howard Chaykin, the six-issue adaptation led directly into a monthly series that lasted 107 issues—ending three years after the release of *Return of the Jedi*! The four-color exploits of the *Star Wars* characters filled the gaps between films thanks to deft writing and careful coordination with Lucasfilm.

The success of the *Star Wars* comics led to a proliferation of licensed Marvel titles, usually adapting other science fiction and fantasy film and TV properties like *Star Trek*, *Logan's Run*, *Dragonslayer*, *Krull*, *Blade Runner* and *Battlestar Galactica*. Marvel also published comics based on James Bond (*For Your Eyes Only*), the Muppets and other Jim Henson productions (*The Muppets Take Manhattan*, *The Dark Crystal*, *Labyrinth*), and toys like *Rom*, *Crystar*, *Strawberry Shortcake*, *Transformers* and *G.I. Joe*. The release of *G.I. Joe* #1 was an industry landmark, part of a major marketing campaign to reintroduce the venerable toy soldier and the subject of the first television commercial devoted to a comic book.

DC Comics also offered media tie-in comics, including new adventures for the *Star Trek* and *Star Trek: The Next Generation* crews as well as adaptations of the live-action TV adventure *Isis*, the toy turned cartoon *Masters of the Universe*, and the *Hot Wheels* toy car line. In 1987-1989, Dark Horse Comics debuted series based on the *Alien* and *Predator* film franchises, pitting the creatures against each other over a decade before they finally met in the movies. Today, film, TV and toy adaptations are still an intrinsic part of the world of comics.

2001: A SPACE ODYSSEY #1
1976. Marvel Comics.

BATTLESTAR GALACTICA #1
1979. Marvel Comics.

G.I. JOE: A REAL AMERICAN HERO #1
1982. Marvel Comics.

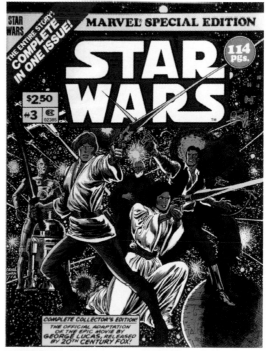

MARVEL SPECIAL EDITION #3
1977. Marvel Comics.

1971 - 1990

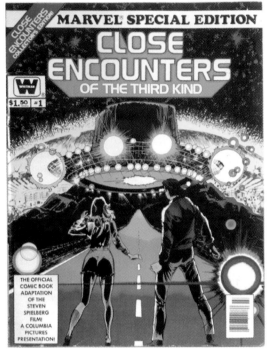

MARVEL SPECIAL EDITION #1
1975. Marvel Comics.

STAR TREK #1
1984. DC Comics.

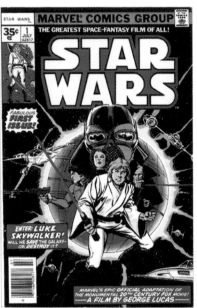

STAR WARS #1
1977. Marvel Comics.

STRAWBERRY SHORTCAKE #1
1985. Marvel Comics.

TRANSFORMERS #1
1984. Marvel Comics.

WELCOME BACK KOTTER #1
1976. DC Comics.

GODZILLA #1
1977. Marvel Comics.

The King of the Monsters was a ferocious symbol of Japan's justifiable fears of atomic destruction, but the giant lizard with the radioactive breath soon became the nation's protector and friend before returning to his villainous roots through almost 30 feature films.

Godzilla (Gojira in Japan) inaugurated the "kaiju" genre of rampaging monster movies that flooded from the east and thrilled the world with its silly but fun combination of rubber-suited actors, exploding model cities and loosely plotted yarns. Godzilla was top of the heap, battling the likes of Ghidrah and Mothra while also finding time to sire a son – the smoke ring-blowing Minya.

Godzilla's first appearance was in 1954's *Godzilla*, which featured actor Raymond Burr in footage spliced in for the film's American release. The many denizens of Monster Island turned up in numerous movies, books, comics, television shows and an endless parade of toys. By the 1970s, Godzilla and his scaly colleagues were multimedia celebrities in their own right.

Godzilla was later reintroduced in a 1984 remake of the first film (again featuring Raymond Burr in the American version), and then again in 1999 for two distinct series of cinematic adventures; a 1998 American movie version was not well received. While he is currently back in hibernation, Godzilla will certainly return to terrorize Tokyo and thrill audiences again and again.

GOING GLOBAL

Jerry: "Hey, an original G.I. Joe with a full Frogman suit!" Girlfriend: "Jerry, what are you doing?" Jerry: "I'm putting this on him and we're going to the sink."
—from Seinfeld, *"The Merv Griffin Show"*

American popular culture of the 1990s to the present was an amalgam of everything that came before, accelerated by a shrinking world of high-speed technology. The widespread adoption of personal computers, the rise of the World Wide Web, Oprah's Book Club, Beanie Babies, music from Spice Girls to Nirvana, Nike sportswear—all these and more characterized this period. Bill Clinton was president through most of the 1990s, television was in 98% of US households, multiplex stadium-seating movie theaters became the norm, and fashion was highly individualistic, from body art (tattoos) to cell phones.

Globalization—cultural, economic and technological exchange—shrank the world even further while creating a greater disparity between "haves" and "have-nots." Science made advances in everything from cloning to space exploration, and CNN brought us 24-hour live coverage of wars and natural disasters, bringing the world home to every American and making us more aware of our fragile place in the scheme of things.

In the ancient world, Man turned to heroes and fictional epics to explain the physical world. Today, we turn to (super)heroes and science (fiction) to explore and describe the world within—the human mind. Popular culture allows us to define our beliefs, to record and interpret our past, and to set goals and dream of the future.

THE SIMPSONS AUTOGRAPHED PICTURE
Circa 1990s. Matt Groening and cast.

THE INCREDIBLES ONE-SHEET
2004. Disney.

VANILLA ICE DOLL
1991. THQ.

MC HAMMER DOLL
1991. Mattel.

221

THE SHI SCULPTURE
Circa 1990s. Moore Creations.

SHREK 2 ETCH A SKETCH
2004. Flair.

TOY STORY EXPRESS TRAIN SET
1996. International Hobby Corp.

POKÉMON: THE FIRST MOVIE #1
1999. Viz Comics.

**THE SPONGEBOB SQUAREPANTS
MOVIE ONE-SHEET**
2004. Nickelodeon Films.

SPOTLIGHT ON...
POKÉMON

At first translated into English as *Pocket Monsters,* the game and franchise that would come to be known as *Pokémon* was created in 1995 and brought to America by Nintendo. The notion of a vast array of tiny critters in an array of colors bred to fight and evolve through constant combat enthralled a generation and helped to cement the handheld Game Boy as the video game device of choice for years to come.

In 1999, Wizards of the Coast issued a trading card game based on the *Pokémon* mythology which was an instant success. To date there are over 250 distinct *Pokémon* characters, with the yellow rabbit-like Pikachu perhaps the most popular and recognizable of them all. Television shows, movies, videos, books, cards and of course an endless array of toys promoted the series, and Pikachu even became a balloon in the Macy's Thanksgiving Day Parade.

The most fascinating aspect of the *Pokémon* craze is that it is virtually identical to the popularity of the Brownies a century earlier. From the one set of spritely characters to the other we can draw a straight line through the 20th century and see the bigger picture of pop culture reflected in sets of iconic creations that capture our hopes and ideals while offering an escape from the pressures of everyday life.

Ultimately, all of these characters are not just entertainment; they are a snapshot of who we are as a people.

WHY ENTERTAINMENT MATTERS

BY ANDREW HERSHBERGER, REGISTRAR

Life is filled with a variety of events that are accorded a gravity disproportionate to our day-to-day accomplishments. Who can argue the Herculean nature of our first step, our first words, our first day of school, our first job, and our first romance? These are moments of our personal legend, recorded and offered to all in books, magazines, photo albums and baby almanacs.

Not as well documented is our development of aesthetic appreciation, that moment when a person discovers what brings them joy. Nebulous as this event might be, it is possibly the most important moment of one's life. When you find out what you enjoy – what entertains you – you can begin life's journey trying to achieve and experience it.

Popular culture is often dismissed as a mere indulgence of the masses. Often when professional critics meet a popular object with approval they will take an apologist's attitude, admitting that they like the item despite their better judgment. The rest of us simply uncheck our enthusiasm, apologize for nothing, and dive headfirst into the community pool.

Though it's been suggested otherwise, popular entertainment is not dominated by (though it's certainly influenced by) media conglomerates. These organizations don't dictate what people will and will not like; entertainment is instead ruled by the public themselves, by what they want and need. Millions of dollars of advertising can lead the public to a film, but it can't make them buy a ticket, and thousands of companies have lost their shirts gambling on the fickle nature of modern society.

Because it's a reflection of what we want to enjoy, popular entertainment is one of the best indicators of a given era's cultural climate, a way to get a sense of who and what we are. Our entertainment distills our moods and tastes and gives them back to us. Through our entertainment we can analyze the mindset of a culture as far back as recorded history and as near as a moment ago.

Our entertainment provides thrills, chills, laughter and tears, and makes us smile or cry or think or even create something ourselves. Our entertainment delights us, directs us, defines us, and definitely makes a difference. Why, entertainment *matters*.

COMIC CHARACTER COLLECTOR CATEGORIES

You've just seen a small sample of our museum collection, and even that is just a taste of the vast scope of American pop culture through the years. We thought it might be interesting to offer a look at the kinds of materials and item categories through which we have come to know and love the many comic characters represented in this book. While they have diverse origins, there's a common thread running through all of these icons, at least those that become the most successful in the long run. It has almost nothing to do with artistic direction, the quality of the material, special effects or the rate of inflation. Instead it has to do with how well that character is marketed to the public.

A character may be introduced by a TV show, a cartoon, a newspaper comic strip, in a comic book, video game or feature film. From any one of these alone a fad, flash-in-the-pan, or short-lived hit may be created, but these things are rarely if ever sustained by only one medium. Instead, it's most often the characters found in the greatest numbers of the categories listed on these two pages that will have the strongest pop culture awareness. Many of the characters seen in this book were the beneficiaries of well-planned marketing and development programs that took them through just about every available medium and type of product.

Using Superman as an example, *Action Comics* #1 launched Superman in comics in 1938. At its peak, the comic book's circulation was approximately 1.5 million copies per month. The Superman daily newspaper strip that debuted in 1939 introduced the Man of Tomorrow to adults and in short order reached 20 million readers. The Superman radio show that premiered in 1940 had 22 million listeners three times a week. So while the comic book was the springboard, it was by no means the only outlet for the Last Son of Krypton. Through club kits, food products, trading cards, apparel, wind-up toys, action figures, watches, live events, posters, standees, radios, telephones and many other products, Superman transcended his relatively humble beginnings to become one of the most recognized characters in the world.

While there are varying levels of achievement for the huge number of characters created since Palmer Cox's success with the Brownies, it's difficult to think of any top characters that are not represented in a significant number of the categories listed on these pages.

Character collectibles have been made from the following materials: Cardboard, Celluloid, Ceramic, Cloth, Glass, Leather, Metal, Paper, Plaster, Plastic, Resin, Rubber, Soap, String, Wood.

Character collectibles have been produced in all of the following categories:

Action figures
Ads
Airplanes
Albums
Ashtrays
Awards
Badges
Balloons
Balls
Bandannas
Banks
Battery toys
Beanbags
Beanie Babies
Beanies
Belts
Big Little Books
Billfolds
Binoculars
Blotters
Bobbing head dolls
Bookmarks
Books
Bottle caps
Bottles
Bowls
Boxes
Bracelets
Bubble bath 'soakies'
Buses
Buttons
Calendars
Cameras
Candles
Candy
Candy containers
Candy machines
Car emblems
Cards
Cars
Casting sets
Catalogues
Cereal box premiums
Cereal boxes
Certificates
Chains
Charms
Christmas cards
Christmas lights
Circus premiums
Clickers
Clocks
Club kits
Coasters
Codebooks
Coins
Colorform sets
Coloring books
Coloring sets
Comic book stands
Comic books
Compasses
Concert programs
Cookie cutters
Cookie jars

Costumes
Coupons
Cracker Jack toys
Crayon sets
Cups
Cut-out books
Decals
Decoders
Detective kits
Dishes
Doll patterns
Dolls
Drawings
Envelopes
Eyeglasses
Fans
Fast food premiums
Figurines
Films
Fishing kits
Flashlights
Flickers
Flip books
Folders
Footwear
Forks
Friction toys
Games
Gasoline premiums
Glasses
Globes
Gloves
Golden books
Greeting cards
Gum cards
Gum wrappers
Gun holsters
Guns
Gyroscopes
Hair accessories
Handbags
Handbills
Handbooks
Handkerchiefs
Hats
Helmets
Ice cream lids
Ingots
Instructions
Jackets
Kaleidoscopes
Key chains
Kites
Knives
Labels
Lamps
Lariats
Leaflets
Letter openers
Letters
License plates
Lighters
Lithographs
Lobby cards
Locks

Lunch bottles
Lunch boxes
Magazines
Magic answer boxes
Magic sets
Magic slates
Magnets
Magnifiers
Mailers
Make-up kits
Manuals
Maps
Marbles
Marionettes
Masks
Matches
Mechanical toys
Medals
Membership cards
Merchandise catalogs
Microscopes
Mirrors
Mobiles
Model kits
Money clips
Movie premiums
Movie programs
Movie viewers
Mugs
Musical instruments
Napkins
Necklaces
Necktie slides
Neckties
Newsletters
Newspaper premiums
Newspapers
Nightlights
Noisemakers
Notepaper
Original art
Ornaments
Package seeds
Paddles
Paint sets
Paper money
Paperbacks
Paper dolls
Paperweights
Party supplies
Patches
Pedometers
Penholders
Pencil boxes
Pencil erasers
Pencil holders
Pencil sharpeners
Pencils
Pennants
Pens
Periscopes
Pez
Phonographs
Photo frames
Photos

Pillows
Pin Wheels
Pinbacks
Pinball Machines
Pins
Pitchers
Placemats
Planters
Plaques
Plates
Play sets
Pocket watches
Pop-up books
Post cards
Posters
Pottery
Press books
Printing sets
Prints
Product containers
Projection equipment
Prototypes
Pull toys
Pulps
Punch-out sets
Punching bags
Puppets
Puzzles
Radio guides
Radio premiums
Radios
Records
Ribbons
Rings
Robots
Rockets

Rugs
Rulers
Salt & pepper shakers
Sandbox toys
Scales
Scarves
School bags
Science kits
Scissors
Scrapbooks
Scripts
Sewing kits
Sheet music
Shirts
Show tickets
Signs
Sirens
Skates
Sleds
Snow domes
Soap
Songbooks
Spaceships
Sparklers
Spinners
Spoons
Sporting goods
Spurs
Squeeze toys
Stamps
Standees
Star finders
Stickers
Stools
Straws
Suspenders

Sweaters
Swords
Tags
Targets
Tattoos
Telephones
Telescopes
Thermometers
Tie bars
Tin containers
Toothbrush holders
Toothbrushes
Tote bags
Toy boats
Toy chests
Toy televisions
Trains
Transfers
Trays
Trucks
TV guides
TV premiums
Umbrellas
Valentines
Videos
Viewers
Walkie-talkies
Wastebaskets
Whistles
Wind-up toys
Wrappers
Wrapping paper
Wristwatches
Writing paper
Yearbooks
Yo-yos

INTO THE FOUR-COLOR WORLD

As you've just read, there are hundreds of categories of successful character items produced over the years, many of them spanning the full period of character toys from the earliest days of the nation through the present. One could easily single out dolls, puzzles, posters or trains among the most enduring examples of successful playthings, and treat them as a museum within a museum. This is what we have done with the American comic book. On the pages that follow, you will see the museum in microcosm through the vibrant colors, inviting formats, and creative energy of comic books. This presentation dovetails precisely with the larger scope of the museum, but offers understanding by singling out this one category of what has been done with incredible characters.

ORIGIN STORY

In the beginning, God made comics, and we drew on the walls of caves trying to tell everybody how we captured a mastodon that afternoon.

—Will Eisner

Although many people believe that reading words alone–prose literature–is a sign of intellectual maturity, the fact is that humans are a visual species, and the blend of words and pictures has always been a natural means of communication that says a great deal about who we are as people. In fact, long before written languages were formalized in any way, at the very dawn of our prehistory, Man explained the world through pictures alone, painting images on cave walls that depicted hunting expeditions or other activities–the world's first comics.

Sequential art used to record history, express cultural beliefs, or tell a story also appears later with Egyptian hieroglyphics–a language based on pictographic forms rather than letters. In Africa and Asia, wood carvings and painted porcelain portrayed scenes of daily life and historical events, again using sequential art to tell the tale. From stained glass windows to the Bayeux Tapestry, there are countless examples of comic-style storytelling throughout human history, testifying to the power of pictures. When written language did emerge, the two methods were often combined, and a medium was born.

Printing technology would transform our relationship with words and pictures and inaugurate the era of true comics, but from the very beginning, comics have been a part of our shared cultural heritage, not just as a nation, but as a species.

A Story
in Four Colors

The more minutely you describe, the more you will confine the mind of the reader, and the more you will keep him from the knowledge of the thing described. And so it is necessary to draw and to describe.
—Leonardo da Vinci

Words and pictures. It's a simple yet powerful combination. Together they can tell tales of triumph and woe, of far-flung futures and distant pasts. They can feature caped heroes and monstrous villains, or just the people next door dealing with ordinary emotions and relationships. Words and pictures combined to make comics can tell any kind of story. They can entertain and educate. Comics are a unique literary art form, and their story is as exciting and enlightening as any featured within the pages of the comic books you will see here.

In this room you will follow the history of comics and sequential art from the dawn of the medium to the early comic books of the 1500s-1800s to the birth of the American comic book industry in the early 1930s and beyond. You'll meet familiar and not-so-familiar faces, learn about some of the creative minds behind the comics, and witness the dark days of the 1950s when a wave of censorship nearly crushed comics out of existence.

Today, comic book characters are a part of our daily lives, appearing on television, in film, on countless household and other products, and even on the Internet. But it all begins on a printed page with words and pictures, a dynamic duo mightier than any superhero.

While it may seem surprising to some that comic books were being published at this time, very early art panels from these eras clearly illustrate the beginnings of the modern comic book as we know it today. The comic strip originated across the ocean hundreds of years before immigrants and importers brought it over to America.

Early examples of comic art during the Pioneer Age include *A Remarkable Story of How Conchine Marquis d'Ancre Was Shot in Paris April 24* (1617). *Buried, Disinterred and Burned. The Burning of Mr. John Rogers* from 1646 is the earliest known North American cartoon printed on paper, and the pamphlet *Plain Truth* from 1747 contains Ben Franklin's earliest known cartoon, *Heaven Helps Only Those Who Help Themselves*, which depicts the ancient superhero Hercules in one corner. These three examples feature sequential art panels similar to modern comic strips.

The Victorian Age began in the United States when the American humor periodical, *Brother Jonathan*, printed the 40-page, 195-panel graphic novel *The Adventures of Obadiah Oldbuck* by Rodolphe Töpffer as a special extra dated September 14, 1842. Other innovations during this period included George Cruikshank's *The Tooth-Ache* in 1849, a sequential story that unfolded accordion-like into a single strip 7 feet 3 inches long. And in the pages of the humor periodical *Wild Oats*, years before he invented the Brownies, Palmer Cox contributed a series of 24-panel comic strips.

By the 1880s, the Victorian Age was coming to an end as the advent of newspaper comic strip reprint books signaled the dawn of the Platinum Age. There is still, however, a lot of overlap between the Victorian and Platinum Ages. The evolution of the American comic strip itself continued in the pages of *Puck*, *Judge*, and *Life* magazines well into the late 1800s.

THE PIONEER AGE
1500s-1828

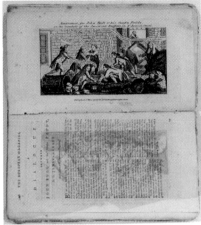

GERMAN BROADSHEET
1569. Unknown publisher.

JOHN BULL AND HIS COUSIN PADDY ILLUSTRATION FROM THE EUROPEAN MAGAZINE AND LONDON REVIEW
1783. Philological Society of London.

THE CORSICAN MUNCHAUSEN ILLUSTRATION BY R. ACKERMANN
1813. The London Strand.

THE VICTORIAN AGE
1828-1883

THE VERITABLE HISTORY OF MR. BACHELOR BUTTERFLY
1845. D. Bogue.

JOURNEY TO THE GOLD DIGGINS BY JEREMIAH SADDLEBAGS
1849. U. P. James.
Coutesy of Steve Meyer.

BROTHER JONATHAN EXTRA #9 CONTAINING THE ADVENTURES OF MR. OBADIAH OLDBUCK
1842. Wilson and Co.
Coutesy of Steve Meyer.

The debut of Palmer Cox's pixie-like Brownies in 1883 also established the form comics would most often take in the Platinum Age—reprint collections of previously published work. Often featuring cardboard covers and varying sizes, comic books such as *Mutt & Jeff*, *Bringing Up Father*, and *The Katzenjammer Kids* drew from popular newspaper strips for their material. The introduction of Richard F. Outcault's Yellow Kid demonstrated the power and potential of a newspaper strip character to increase sales of newspapers and licensed merchandise, an idea pioneered earlier by the Brownies. This led to the publication of Dillingham & Company's 196-page *The Yellow Kid in McFadden's Flats* in 1897.

But it was the debut of *Famous Funnies* #1 in May 1934, with reprints of Sunday strips *Toonerville Folks*, *Mutt & Jeff*, *Hairbreadth Harry*, *S'Matter Pop*, *Nipper*, *Dixie Dugan*, *Tailspin Tommy*, *The Nebbs*, *Joe Palooka* and many more, that introduced the monthly newsstand magazine format that would become the dominant form of American comic books for decades to come.

While the future of comics was being made, other formats often seen as predecessors or cousins to the comic book were also vying for attention, including pulps like *Argosy Magazine*, *Weird Tales*, and *Spicy Mystery*. Pulp periodicals showcased future comic book stars Tarzan, Doc Savage, Conan and The Shadow.

Another popular format was Big Little Books, which featured adaptations of newspaper strips but with large, easy-to-read text accompanying single panel illustrations.

By the end of the Platinum Age, the comic book format only lacked an iconic figure that would rocket its popularity to new heights, and he was about to arrive from a doomed planet.

BUSTER BROWN AND HIS RESOLUTIONS

1903. Frederick A. Stokes Co. First nationally distributed comic.

PORE LI'L MOSE HIS LETTERS TO HIS MAMMY

1902. Cupples & Leon. Earliest Cupples & Leon comic.

THE ILLUSTRATED TARZAN BOOK #1

1929. Grosset & Dunlap. Second printing.

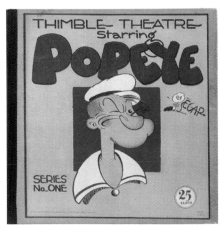

THIMBLE THEATRE STARRING POPEYE SERIES #1

1931. Sonnet Publishing. Origin retold.

TILLIE THE TOILER BOOK #7

1932. Cupples & Leon.

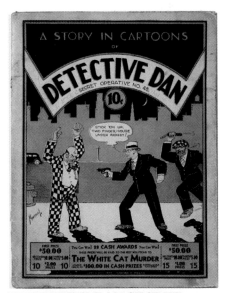

DETECTIVE DAN SECRET OPERATIVE NO. 48

1933. Humor Publishing. One of the first comics with original art and a single theme.

NEW FUN COMICS #1
1935. DC Comics. First DC comic.

ACE COMICS #1
1937. David McKay Publications.

NEW COMICS #1
1935. DC Comics.

BRINGING UP FATHER

George McManus' comic strip first appeared in 1913 and introduced readers to an Irish-American family whose lives are drastically altered by winning the grand prize in an Irish sweepstakes. Jiggs would prefer to maintain a simple life, while his wife Maggie and daughter Nora yearn for social acceptance. McManus' characters were widely embraced, and by 1916 *Bringing Up Father* began appearing as a daily strip; Sunday strips began nationwide in April 1918.

Pot-bellied Jiggs was comfortably familiar to his working class audience with his desire to keep his family grounded, hanging out with

DETECTIVE COMICS #1
1937. DC Comics.

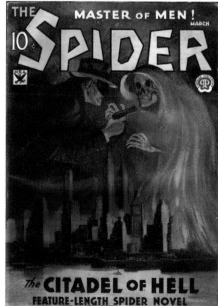

THE SPIDER VOL. 2 #2
1934. Popular Publications.

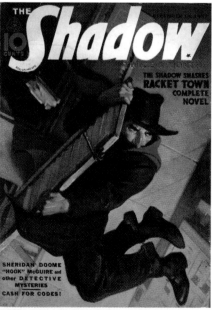

THE SHADOW VOL. XXIV #2
1937. Street & Smith Publications.

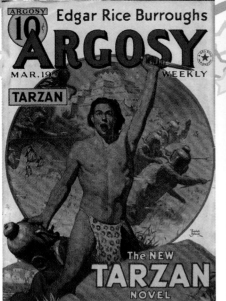

ARGOSY
1938. Frank A. Munsey Company.
March 19 issue.

WINGS VOL. IX #10
1944. Wings Publishing.

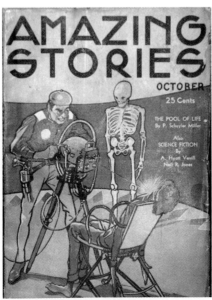

THRILLING LOVE VOL. LXX #1
1949. Standard Magazine.

his restaurant-owning friend Dinty Moore and eating traditional "poor man's cuisine" like cabbage and corned beef. Maggie's attempts to transcend her humble heritage also rang true in the pre-Depression era when new money made for new (and in Maggie's case, snooty) attitudes.

Bringing Up Father's appeal spread pretty quickly from print to stage to screen, but oddly, it never became a comic book success. After McManus died in 1954, the strip was continued by many talented illustrators. By the time Jiggs and Maggie adorned a US postage stamp in 1995 and appeared in their final strip on May 28, 2000, *Bringing Up Father* had become the longest running daily strip ever.

FANTASTIC ADVENTURES VOL. 13 #7
1951. Ziff-Davis Publishing.

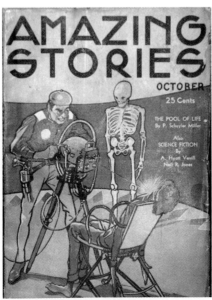

AMAZING STORIES #1
1926. October Issue.

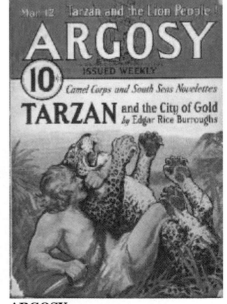

ARGOSY
1938. Frank A. Munsey Company.
March 12 issue.

First published in 1932, Big Little Books were even more popular than other comic books during their heyday. Whitman Publishing Co. was the first to establish the format—short, stubby hardcover and softcover books costing just 10 or 15 cents and featuring adaptations of newspaper strips with large, easy-to-read text accompanying single panel illustrations often taken from the strips themselves. Soon other companies were publishing books in a wide range of similar styles. Throughout the '30s and '40s, Big Little Books reigned supreme until finally, comics surpassed them and never looked back.

Whitman's Big Little Book line was launched with *The Adventures of Dick Tracy* and was quickly followed by books featuring Mickey Mouse, Little Orphan Annie, Buck Rogers, Flash Gordon and many more. As the books proliferated, they adapted radio and film stories as well as original material in addition to newspaper strip reprints. For just a dime, kids could read about the exploits of their favorite characters in a format fit for their pocket both physically and financially.

Sadly, the post-war years weren't kind to the Big Little Books or their competitors as television proved a more enticing entertainment option for children. The media that had provided most of the inspiration for the content of Big Little Books—newspapers and radio—also waned in influence. Short-term revivals, sometimes adding features like "Flip-it" pictures in the page corners, failed to recapture their early success. By the early 1980s, Big Little Books had all but vanished.

In the 1990s, however, Chronicle Books released a short series of familiar TV and film tie-in hardcovers, Mighty Chronicles, featuring adaptations of the *Star Wars* movies and the *Hercules* and *Xena* television series. These new Big Little Books were designed to look almost identical to their 1930s ancestors inside and out, but instead of a 10-cent cover price, the new books cost 10 dollars each. Such is progress.

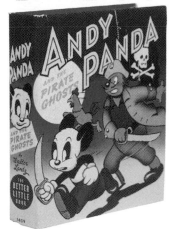

ANDY PANDA AND THE PIRATE GHOSTS
1949. Whitman Publishing #1459.

(WALT DISNEY'S) BAMBI
1942. Whitman Publishing #1469.

BLONDIE AND DAGWOOD IN HOT WATER
1946. Whitman Publishing #1410.

BUCK ROGERS IN THE 25TH CENTURY A.D.
1933. Whitman Publishing #742.

BUGS BUNNY ALL PICTURES COMICS
1944. Whitman Publishing #1435.

CAPTAIN MIDNIGHT AND SHEIK JOMAK KHAN
1946. Whitman Publishing #1402.

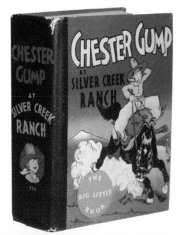

CHESTER GUMP AT SILVER CREEK RANCH
1933. Whitman Publishing #734.

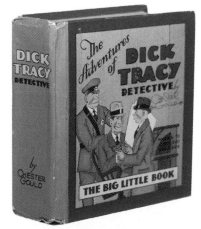

THE ADVS. OF DICK TRACY
1933. Whitman Publishing. First Big Little Book.

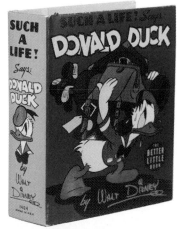

SUCH A LIFE! SAYS: DONALD DUCK
1939. Whitman Publishing #1404.

FLASH GORDON IN THE ICE WORLD OF MONGO
1942. Whitman Publishing #1443.

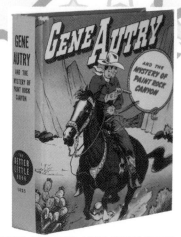

GENE AUTRY AND THE MYS-TERY OF PAINT ROCK CANYON
1947. Whitman Publishing #1425.

THE GREEN HORNET CRACKS DOWN
1942. Whitman Publishing #1480.

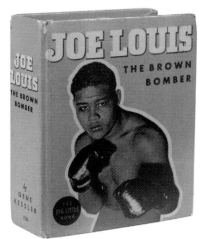

JOE LOUIS THE BROWN BOMBER
1936. Whitman Publishing #1105.

THE LAUGHING DRAGON OF OZ
1934. Whitman Publishing #1126. Very rare due to a legal dispute that led to a single print run and the destruction of many copies.

LITTLE ORPHAN ANNIE
1933. Whitman Publishing #708. Second Big Little Book.

THE LONE RANGER AND THE BLACK SHIRT HIGHWAYMAN
1939. Whitman Publishing #1450.

MANDRAKE THE MAGICIAN AND THE FLAME PEARLS
1946. Whitman Publishing #1418.

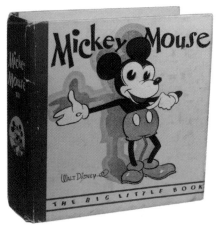

MICKEY MOUSE
1933. Whitman Publishing #717.

MICKEY MOUSE
1933. Whitman Publishing #717.
Second printing with different cover.

MICKEY MOUSE THE MAIL PILOT
1933. Whitman Publishing #731.
Very rare second printing of "The Mail Pilot" with modified cover from #717.

THE PHANTOM AND DESERT JUSTICE
1941. Whitman Publishing #1421.

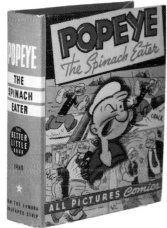

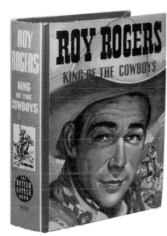

POPEYE THE SPINACH EATER ALL PICTURES COMICS
1945. Whitman Publishing #1480.

ROY ROGERS KING OF THE COWBOYS
1943. Whitman Publishing #1476.

THE SHADOW AND THE MASTER OF EVIL
1941. Whitman Publishing #1443.

(WALT DISNEY'S) SNOW WHITE AND THE SEVEN DWARFS
1938. Whitman Publishing #1460.

TARZAN IN THE LAND OF THE GIANT APES
1949. Whitman Publishing #1467.

TOM SWIFT AND HIS MAGNET-IC SILENCER
1941. Whitman Publishing #1437.

Beginning with the introduction of Superman in *Action Comics* #1 (June 1938), the Golden Age established the superhero genre as the dominant form of comic book storytelling in America. Previously filled with newspaper reprints, comics were now featuring original material, and superheroes led the way into a new era. Superman's whirlwind popularity led to the debut of many other heroes on the newsstands. Batman appeared a year later in *Detective Comics* #27, followed by Captain Marvel, Captain America, The Flash, Green Lantern, Wonder Woman, The Sub-Mariner, Mary Marvel, The Spectre, The Human Torch, and many more. A veritable army of super-beings arrived just in time to usher the nation into the dark but ultimately triumphant days of World War II.

But the superheroes weren't alone. Throughout the Golden Age, other beloved characters made their first comic book appearances, from Disney and Warner Bros. cartoon stars like Donald Duck and Bugs Bunny, to Archie, Veronica, Betty, Jughead and the rest of their teenaged pals, to western adventurers like the Lone Ranger, Roy Rogers and Gene Autry. Many of these comics boasted circulation numbers of over a million copies a month. Soon newsstands were filled to overflowing with four-color fantasies of nearly every genre imaginable.

The superheroes may have seemed invincible, but with the end of World War II came the end of their reign...for the time being. No longer fueled by patriotic fervor and the need to rally forces at home and abroad, the superhero genre was now a bit passé, and in an effort to boost sales comics would begin to tell ever more shocking stories without caped crusaders. In making this change, the medium would face perhaps the greatest challenge in its history, and it would do so without the help of the brightly garbed heroes who once carried the comic book banner into the stratosphere.

ACTION COMICS #1
1938. DC Comics. Court copy.

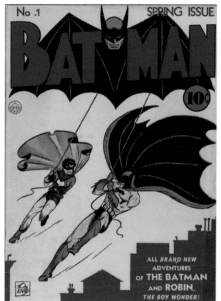

BATMAN #1
1940. DC Comics.

CAPTAIN AMERICA COMICS #1
1941. Timely Comics.

**CAPTAIN MARVEL
ADVENTURES #51**
1946. Fawcett Publications.

DETECTIVE COMICS #27
1939. DC Comics.

DOUBLE ACTION COMICS #2
1940. DC Comics.

FOUR COLOR #48
1944. Dell Publishing.

FOUR COLOR #74
1945. Dell Publishing.

FOUR COLOR #86
1945. Dell Publishing.

ARCHIE ANDREWS

The Golden Age may seem like it was all capes and tights, but when *Pep Comics* #22 introduced eternal teenager Archie Andrews, the redhead held his own against the likes of Superman and the Sub-Mariner. In 1942, Archie made the leap to his own title. In the 60 years since, Archie has been featured in more than 30 different titles, on radio, and in cartoons, movies and TV shows. He's appeared on cereal boxes, pinbacks, magazines, calendars, and other character collectibles. The comics even inspired the creation of The Archies, a pop group that scored a couple of hit records like "Sugar, Sugar," originally intended for the

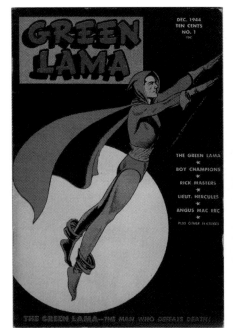

GREEN LAMA #1
1944. Spark Publications.

MARVEL COMICS #1
1939. Timely Comics.

MASTER COMICS #27
1942. Fawcett Publications.

NEW YORK WORLD'S FAIR
1940. DC Comics.

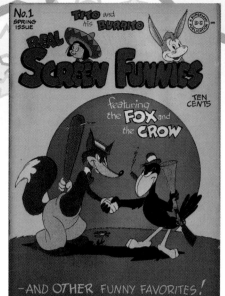

REAL SCREEN FUNNIES #1
1945. DC Comics.

SENSATION COMICS #1
1942. DC Comics.

Monkees, and in turn inspired another cartoon interpretation of the characters.

Archie has spawned spin-offs like *Josie & The Pussycats* and *Sabrina The Teenage Witch* as well as variations like *Archie's Weird Mysteries*, a *Scooby Doo / The X-Files* take on the characters. He's even met Marvel Comics' Punisher and lived to tell the tale! Through it all though, Archie has been largely untouched by the changing culture and remains what he always was – wholesome family entertainment. Archie, obnoxious rival Reggie, hungry buddy Jughead, girl-next-door Betty, and socialite Veronica will always be there in the Rockwellian small town paradise of Riverdale, USA.

WALT DISNEY'S COMICS AND STORIES #1
1940. Dell Publishing.

WALT DISNEY'S COMICS AND STORIES #46
1944. Dell Publishing.

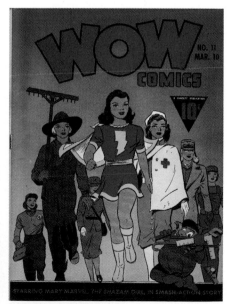

WOW COMICS #11
1943. Fawcett Publications.

Special purpose comics, giveaways, premiums—whatever you call them, there has always been a category of comic books published specifically to promote an idea, a product, a person or even other comics. Often offered for free with action figures or video games, or as mail-away premiums with proofs of purchase from a particular product, these comics serve a practical purpose.

Premium comics have swayed elections (*The Story of Harry Truman*, 1948), solicited for charities (*Donald Duck and the Red Feather*, 1948), discouraged kids from smoking (*Captain America Meets the Asthma Monster*, 1987), pleaded for social justice (*Consumer Comics*, 1975), discussed the environment (*Our Spaceship Earth*, 1947), taught history (*Louisiana Purchase*, 1953), explained computers (*Superman Radio Shack Giveaway*, 1980), hammered Communism (*How Stalin Hopes to Destroy America*, 1951), fought discrimination (*Mammy Yokum & the Great Dogpatch Mystery*, 1956), encouraged literacy (*Linus Gets a Library Card*, 1960), recruited for the armed forces (*Li'l Abner Joins the Navy,* 1950), and explained birth control (*Escape from Fear*, 1950, later revised).

As early as the April 1933 issue of *Fortune Magazine*, the business world recognized the power of comics to communicate as well as entertain, noting that over $1 million dollars was spent in 1932 for advertising space in newspapers adjacent to the funny pages. In the years to come, promotional comics of all types would become a mainstay of the industry, pairing superheroes, funny animals and other characters with social, political, and cultural topics from banking to drug addiction.

As long as consumers are enticed by a free gift, premium comics will remain a useful promotional tool as well as another weapon in the war against misconceptions about the true power of the comics medium.

PROMOTIONAL COMICS

ADVENTURES OF BIG BOY #1
1956. Timely Comics.

ADVENTURES OF SUPERMAN
Circa 1940s. DC Comics.

ARCHIE AND FRIENDS: MONSTER BASH 2003
2003. Archie Comics.

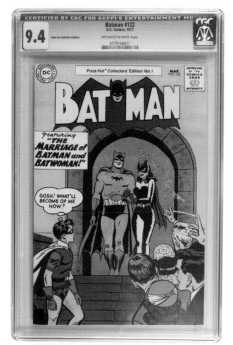

BATMAN #122 PIZZA HUT EDITION
1977. DC Comics.

BLOOD IS THE HARVEST
1950. Catechetical Guild.

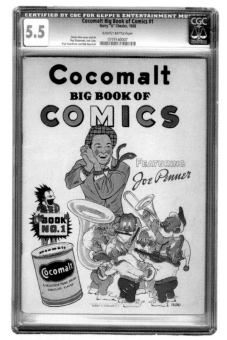

COCOMALT BIG BOOK OF COMICS
1938. Harry "A" Chesler.

DONALD AND MICKEY MERRY CHRISTMAS
1948. Firestone Tire & Rubber Co.

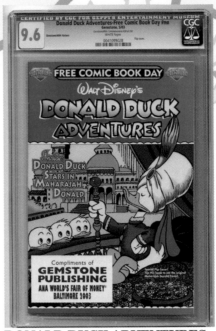

DONALD DUCK ADVENTURES FCBD EDITION
2003. Gemstone Publishing

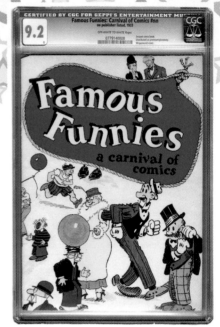

FAMOUS FUNNIES
1934. Eastern Color Printing Co.

THE SPIRIT

A pioneer of the American comic book industry, Will Eisner developed his own comic magazine insert for newspapers, a collection of strips including his most famous crime-fighting creation, *The Spirit*. *The Spirit* sections ran in newspapers across the United States from 1941 to 1952, reaching up to about 5 million readers every Sunday.

The Spirit stories from these sections are still considered revolutionary in their design.

The non-standard *Spirit* logo was generally worked into the opening visual in a powerful way, and Eisner was not a prisoner of standard panel-per-page counts.

Eisner was absent from he strip between 1942-1945 while he served during World War II

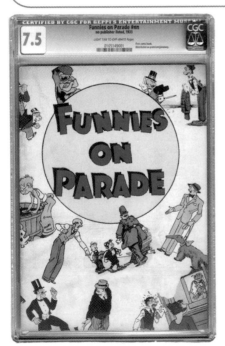

FUNNIES ON PARADE
1933. Eastern Color Printing Co.

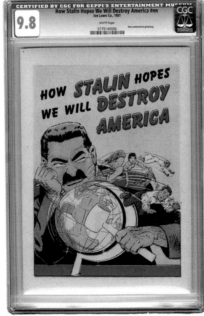

HOW STALIN HOPES WE WILL DESTROY AMERICA
1951. Joe Lowe Co.

KITE FUN BOOK
1954. Sou. California Edison Co.

LONE RANGER IN MILK FOR BIG MIKE
1955. Dell Publishing.

THE SPIRIT SECTION
1941. Will Eisner.

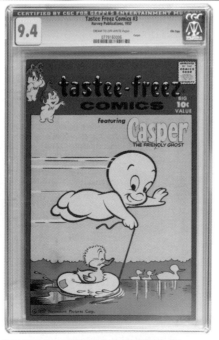

THE STORY OF INFLATION
2001. Federal Reserve Bank.

and again toward the end of the strip when other creators such as EC Comics' Wally Wood served as illustrator. Although it ended in 1952, *The Spirit* has regularly been reprinted as it finds appeal with successive generations.

Publishers like Quality Comics, Fiction House, Harvey Comics, Kitchen Sink Press, Warren Publications and DC Comics have released comic book versions of the strips since the mid-1940s, attesting to the ongoing popularity of Eisner's creation.

The Spirit is even poised to make his long-awaited debut on the silver screen, continuing his crusade for justice well into the 21st century.

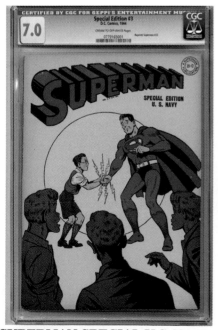

SUPERMAN SPECIAL U.S. NAVY EDITION #3
1944. DC Comics.

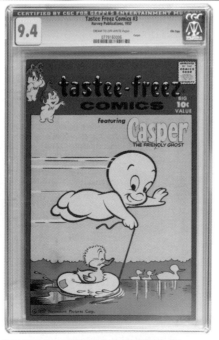

TASTEE FREEZ COMICS #3
1957. Harvey Publications.

YOU'VE GOT TO HAVE GRIT
1959. Grit Publishing Co.

With the decline in sales suffered by superhero comics after the end of World War II, comic book publishers turned to genres like crime, horror, science fiction, and romance to save the day. Topping one another with increasingly intense artwork and stories, the comics of this era featured such horrific tableaux as hangings, decapitations, electrocutions, drug use, and torture; women were often the victims. Soon enough, the industry drew unwanted attention for the severity of its content.

These comics attracted the likes of Dr. Frederic Wertham, whose book *Seduction of the Innocent* laid the blame for America's "adolescent bandits" entirely at the feet of the comic book industry. With public outcry growing across the nation, fuelled by fear-mongering articles in *Woman's Day*, *Saturday Review*, *Parent's*, and local newspapers, Senator Estes Kefauver and his Senate Subcommittee on Juvenile Delinquency began to investigate the comic book industry. William Gaines, publisher of the notorious EC Comics line–the source for much of Wertham's argument against comics with series like *Tales From the Crypt*, *Vault of Horror*, *Crime SuspenStories*, and *Weird Science-Fantasy*–testified before the committee. In the end, the comic book publishers themselves took action rather than watch their business collapse.

The Comics Code Authority was established in 1954 to regulate the content of all comics published with its cover seal. Oddly enough, just about everything EC Comics published was now forbidden by the Code apart from their humor magazine, *MAD*, and the gory excesses of the era came sharply to an end.

Other comic categories like Disney, funny animal, western, movie, TV and teenaged titles had flourished during this period as well, but this ten-year Age would prove to be only a short respite before the superheroes returned to reclaim their throne.

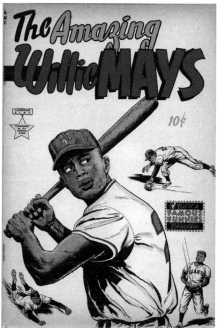

THE AMAZING WILLIE MAYS
1954. Famous Funnies.

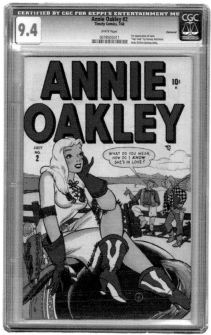

ANNIE OAKLEY #2
1948. Timely Comics.

ARCHIE'S GIRLS BETTY & VE-RONICA #1
1950. Archie Publications.

ATOMIC WAR! #1
1952. Ace Periodicals.

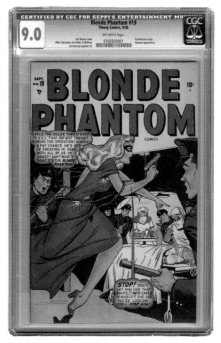

BLONDE PHANTOM #19
1948. Timely Comics.

CASPER #1
1948. Harvey Comics.

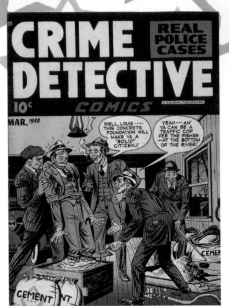

CRIME DETECTIVE COMICS #1
1948. Hillman Periodicals.

THE DEAD WHO WALK
1952. Realistic Comics.

FOUR COLOR #535
1954. Dell Publishing.

CASPER & RICHIE RICH

The amiable apparition known as Casper was first spotted in a 1945 Famous Studios "Noveltoon" cartoon called *The Friendly Ghost*. Created by Seymour V. Reit and Joe Oriolo, Casper resurfaced three years later in *There's Good Boos Tonight*. Soon his ghost-against-type personality made him the star of his own full-blown series as well as a plethora of comics produced by St. John Publishing beginning in 1949. Harvey Comics took over Casper's chronicles in 1952.

Harvey must have empathized with the translucent little guy for he was given an admittedly troublesome family at Harvey dubbed the

FOUR COLOR #629
1955. Dell Publishing.

GIRLS IN LOVE #46
1955. Quality Comics Group.

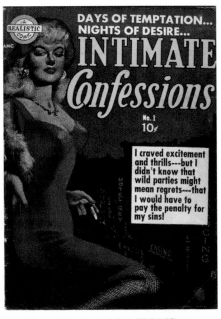

INTIMATE CONFESSIONS #1
1951. Realistic Comics.

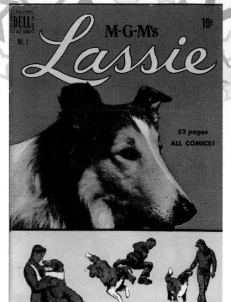

LASSIE #1
1950. Dell Publishing.

MYSTERY IN SPACE #1
1951. DC Comics.

PEANUTS #1
1953-1954. Dell Publishing.

Ghostly Trio; a horse, Nightmare; and a nemesis, Spooky the Tough Little Ghost. Casper also found a long-lasting friend in Wendy the Good Little Witch, a Harvey Comics star in her own right.

The Harvey characters delighted children for decades, with a universe of little adventurers that included the wealthy wandering soul, Richie Rich, the gluttonous Little Lotta and the circle-obsessed Little Dot. Casper and Richie Rich alone accounted for an impressive number of separate comic series, and both characters even made it to the big time with live-action feature films in 1994 (*Richie Rich* starring Macaulay Culkin) and 1995 (Casper co-starring Christina Ricci).

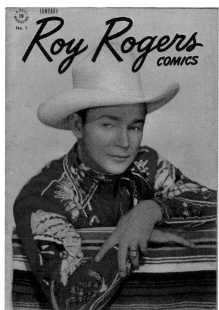

ROY ROGERS COMICS #1
1948. Dell Publishing.

SUPERBOY #1
1949. DC Comics.

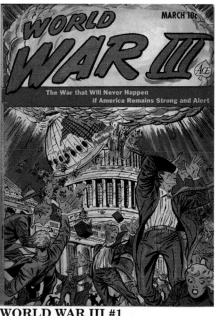

WORLD WAR III #1
1953. Ace Periodicals.

Gather around, kiddies! It's time for a ghoulish tale of monsters, murder, and mayhem–the shocking story of...EC Comics! Originally founded as Educational (later Entertainment) Comics, EC made its mark when publisher William Gaines collaborated with artists Al Feldstein, Johnny Craig, Johnny Severin, Wally Wood and Bill Elder to introduce new comics with crime and romance stories.

The "New Trend" EC titles debuted in 1950, blending socio-political commentary with provocative, often violent subject matter. Their biggest success was in horror and sci-fi, with anthologies like *Tales From the Crypt*, *Vault of Horror* and *Weird Science-Fantasy*. Mixing gory artwork with macabre tales hosted by the likes of the Crypt Keeper and the Old Witch, the new EC was a sensation in every sense of the word.

But EC fell victim to a witch-hunt in 1954 when American public opinion turned against comics thanks to the efforts of Dr. Frederic Wertham and Senator Estes Kefauver. Targeting comics as a major cause of juvenile delinquency, a Senate subcommittee condemned EC and inspired the other comic book publishers to create their own internal censorship code to prevent further investigation–the Comics Code Authority.

The Code sealed EC's fate. EC introduced a "New Direction" set of titles in 1955 like *Impact*, *M.D.*, and *Psychoanalysis*, but the end was near. EC's one remaining success–a humor series called *MAD*–escaped the Code by transforming into a magazine still published today.

During their short-lived reign, EC Comics pushed the boundaries of what was acceptable and demonstrated the potential of the comics medium to provoke thought and tackle heavier subject matter with tongue planted firmly in cheek. To coin a cliché, comics would never be the same again.

Another dead-time story, kiddies?

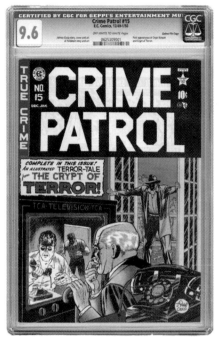

CRIME PATROL #15
1949-1950. EC Comics.

CRIME SUSPENSTORIES #1
1950. EC Comics.

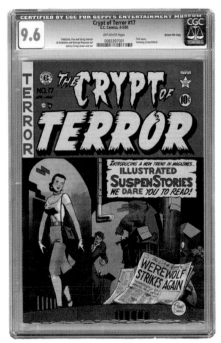

CRYPT OF TERROR #17
1950. EC Comics.

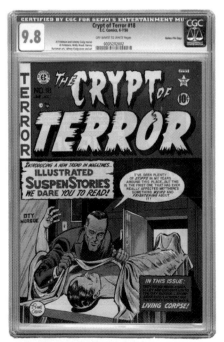

CRYPT OF TERROR #18
1950. EC Comics.

CRYPT OF TERROR #19
1950. EC Comics.

FRONTLINE COMBAT #1
1951. EC Comics.

EC COLLECTION

HAUNT OF FEAR #15 (#1)
1950. EC Comics.

HAUNT OF FEAR #16 (#2)
1950. EC Comics.

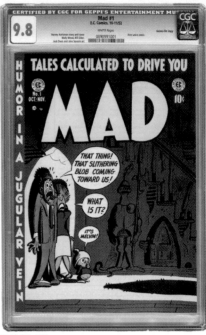

MAD #1
1952. EC Comics.

THE FOUR EC HOSTS

Fans of classic EC Comics *Tales from the Crypt, Vault of Horror* and *The Haunt of Fear* are all familiar with their respective 'hosts,' the Crypt Keeper, the Vault Keeper and the Old Witch, but few know of Drusilla, the buxom brunette who appeared as the Vault Keeper's assistant and was to be host of the never-published *Vault of Terror.*

This black-clad Elvira-esque character never appeared on any EC covers but can be seen in the background of the 30th edition cover of *The Official Overstreet Comic Book Price Guide.*

The Crypt Keeper is by far the most infamous EC host, well known to modern fans

MAD #24
1955. EC Comics.

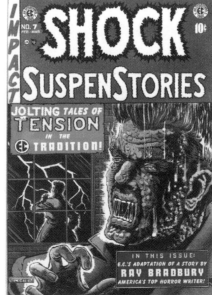

SHOCK SUSPENSTORIES #7
1953. EC Comics.

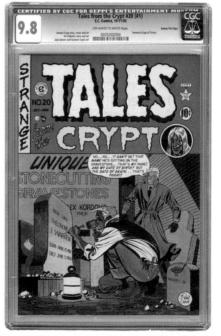

TALES FROM THE CRYPT #20 (#1)
1950. EC Comics.

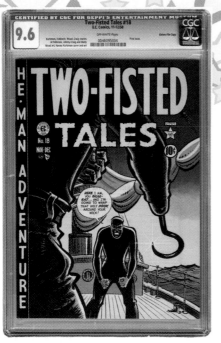

TWO-FISTED TALES #18 (#1)
1950. EC Comics.

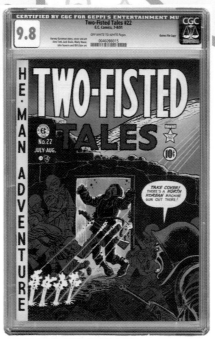

TWO-FISTED TALES #22
1951. EC Comics.

VAULT OF HORROR #12 (#1)
1950. EC Comics.

from his duties as host of the HBO cable television incarnation of *Tales from the Crypt* aired in the 1990s. From his haunting laugh and twisted sense of humor to his decomposing body, the revamped Crypt Keeper truly "resur-

rected" a classic character and introduced a new generation to his terrifying tales.

As for the Vault Keeper and the Old Witch, while never gaining as much notoriety as the Crypt Keeper they both still managed to entertain

readers from month to month with their stories of the macabre, their chilling introductions and their insidious commentary. Together with the Crypt Keeper, they made up an "unholy trinity" of horror hosts. Poor Drusilla.

WAR AGAINST CRIME! #10
1950. EC Comics.

WEIRD SCIENCE #6
1951. EC Comics.

WEIRD SCIENCE #7
1951. EC Comics.

Superheroes streaked back into comics with a vengeance when a new version of DC's The Flash, last seen in 1949, debuted in *Showcase* #4 in 1956. Technically, superheroes had never entirely gone away, but their popularity had reached a low ebb when DC Comics editor Julius Schwartz decided to revamp several Golden Age heroes for a new, more scientific era. Green Lantern, Aquaman, The Atom, Hawkman, Supergirl and The Spectre followed, with old-timers Superman, Batman and Wonder Woman welcoming their colleagues back to comics. *The Justice League of America* (1960) offered a chance for fans to see their heroes teaming up to preserve justice, just as they had done 20 years earlier as the Justice Society in the pages of *All-Star Comics*.

If the DC superhero revival was a turning point, however, the birth of the "Marvel Age of Comics" with *Fantastic Four* #1 in November 1961 was nothing less than a seismic shift. Fuelled by the creative genius of Stan Lee, Jack Kirby, Steve Ditko, and a bullpen of creators ready to create a new universe of more human superheroes, Marvel Comics introduced the notion of superheroic characters with familiar desires and foibles as well as more technologically based origins. The result was an instant connection with a generation of comic book readers who eagerly snapped up every issue of titles like *The Incredible Hulk*, *The X-Men*, *Daredevil*, *The Avengers*, and of course, *The Amazing Spider-Man*.

Marvel quickly supplanted DC as the cultural center of the superhero comic book movement during this time, although Batman benefited from the debut of his campy late '60s television series. The Silver Age represented not only a rebirth for superheroes but the beginning of a lengthy reign for the genre as the most popular and recognizable form of American comic book storytelling.

ACTION COMICS #252
1959. DC Comics.

AMAZING FANTASY #15
1962. Marvel Comics.

AMAZING SPIDER-MAN #1
1962. Marvel Comics.

THE AVENGERS #4
1964. Marvel Comics.

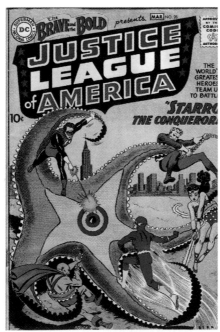

THE BRAVE AND THE BOLD #28
1960. DC Comics.

FANTASTIC FOUR #1
1961. Marvel Comics.

1956 - 1970

THE FLASH #123
1961. DC Comics.

THE JETSONS #23
1967. Gold Key.

THE INCREDIBLE HULK #1
1962. Marvel Comics.

THE FLASH

With a bolt of lightning and a splash of chemicals, the Flash blazed into the DC Universe with all the power of the Speed Force. Created by Julius Schwartz and Carmine Infantino, this revamped version of the Golden Age character first debuted in DC's *Showcase* #4 in 1956.

After a freak accident during a thunderstorm, police scientist Barry Allen found that he could move near the speed of light. Inspired by the earlier Flash, Jay Garrick, Allen took on the moniker and soon became a celebrated hero.

But Barry Allen was destined to become a hero on two fronts. Aside from becoming one of the greatest heroes

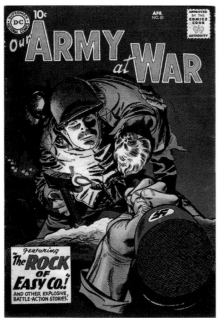

OUR ARMY AT WAR #81
1959. DC Comics.

RICHIE RICH #1
1960. Harvey Comics.

SHOWCASE #4
1956. DC Comics.

SHOWCASE #22
1959. DC Comics.

STAR TREK #1
1967. Gold Key.

**SUPERMAN'S GIRLFRIEND
LOIS LANE #1**
1958. DC Comics.

of the Silver Age, a founding member of the Justice League of America, and the fastest man alive, Allen also became a hero to the comic book industry. The Flash's re-emergence breathed new life into the superhero genre and inspired many other Silver Age revivals of DC characters.

Allen faced a lot of tragedy for a superhero, from the death of his beloved wife, Iris, at the hands of the evil Captain Zoom, to his supreme sacrifice during 1985's *Crisis on Infinite Earths*, in which he gave his life to save the multiverse and became one with the Speed Force.

Although others have since inherited the mantle of the Flash, some believe Barry Allen will one day run again.

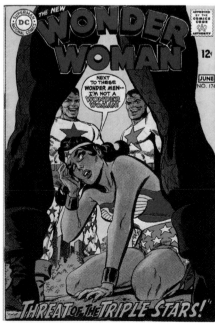

WONDER WOMAN #176
1968. DC Comics.

THE X-MEN #1
1963. Marvel Comics.

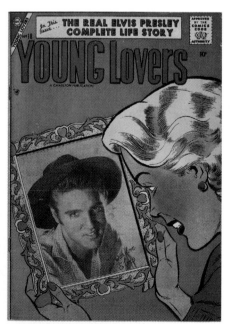

YOUNG LOVERS #18
1957. Charlton Comics.

With age comes wisdom. Now entering their fourth decade, American comic book superheroes were showing a new maturity with stories that reflected more socially relevant themes and a willingness to push boundaries. But first, the legacy of the 1950s censorship of comics—the Comics Code Authority—had to change with the times.

The first major assault on the Code occurred when Marvel released an *Amazing Spider-Man* story about drug addiction without the Code's approval. Only a few months later, DC followed with its own anti-drug story in *Green Lantern*, but this time the seal was present.

Green Lantern/Green Arrow #76, written by Denny O'Neil, featured a story in which racial issues were dealt with bluntly, and soon superheroes were battling for justice against cultural threats equally as challenging as those posed by monsters and madmen.

Marvel's universe was expanding rapidly. 1975 saw the reintroduction of Marvel's *X-Men*, with new hero Wolverine. The Punisher was a vigilante who fought evil with bullets instead of fanciful powers. Luke Cage was an African-American hero who offered his abilities for hire. And in an ancient land of swords and sorcery, Conan the Barbarian wandered the land seeking adventure.

Other debuts included *Swamp Thing*, *Micronauts*, *The Defenders*, and the return of the original Captain Marvel in *Shazam* #1 (1973). Independent publishers like Mirage, Pacific, Comico, Eclipse and Warp premiered *Cerebus*, *Elfquest*, *Sabre* and *Teenage Mutant Ninja Turtles*. By the early 1980s, the Direct Market and comic shops around the country led to another explosion of publishers and titles in a variety of genres, but always with superheroes leading the way to store shelves.

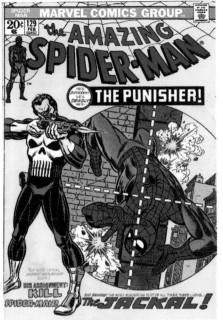

AMAZING SPIDER-MAN #129
1974. Marvel Comics.

BLACK LIGHTNING #1
1977. DC Comics.

THE CAT #1
1972. Marvel Comics.

CEREBUS THE AARDVARK #1
1977. Aardvark-Vanaheim.

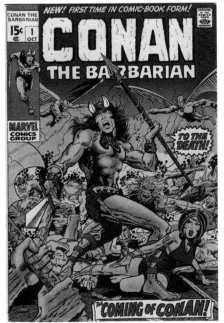

CONAN THE BARBARIAN #1
1970. Marvel Comics.

**THE DARK MANSION OF
FORBIDDEN LOVE #1**
1971. DC Comics.

1970 - 1984

261

ELFQUEST #1
1979. Warp Graphics.

GHOST RIDER #1
1973. Marvel Comics.

GIANT-SIZE X-MEN #1
1975. Marvel Comics.

WOLVERINE

In 1974, Marvel Comics introduced fans to a character that would soon become the company's most popular creation since its birth in 1961. In the pages of *The Incredible Hulk*

#180-181, creators Len Wein and John Romita Sr. pitted the Green Goliath against "the greatest Canadian super-hero," Wolverine. With a mutant ability to heal and razor-sharp adamantium claws, he was an instant hit.

Wolverine was reintroduced in 1975's *Giant Size X-Men* #1, with writer Dave Cockrum and artist Gil Kane establishing him as a member of the revitalized mutant team. Soon he was a ubiquitous presence in the Marvel universe, a violent anti-

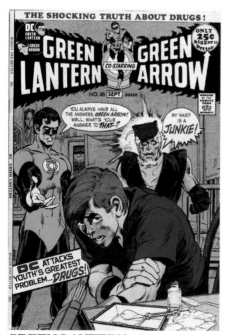

GREEN LANTERN #85
1971. DC Comics.

THE INCREDIBLE HULK #181
1974. Marvel Comics.

THE NEW TEEN TITANS #1
1980. DC Comics.

THE SAVAGE SHE-HULK #1
1980. DC Comics.

THE SHADOW #1
1973. DC Comics.

SHAZAM! #1
1973. DC Comics.

hero whose past was a mystery but whose future of fan popularity was assured.

In 2001, Marvel delved into Wolverine's early life in the mini-series *Origin*, establishing that he was born as James Howlett, the second son of John and Elizabeth Howlett in 19th century Alberta. After the brutal murder of his family by Thomas and Dog Logan, James and his one-time love, Rose, went into exile in the Canadian wilderness. Adopting the name Logan, Howlett was later taken for a secret government project called Weapon X, where his bones were surgically laced with adamantium.

Today Wolverine is even more well known thanks to the *X-Men* films, where he is played by Hugh Jackman.

SUPERMAN #233
1971. DC Comics.

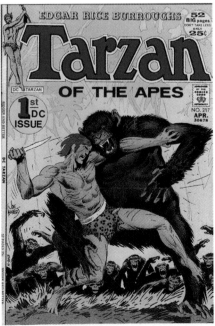

TARZAN #207
1972. DC Comics.

TOMB OF DRACULA #10
1973. Marvel Comics.

As American comic books entered their fifth decade, the mainstream media was starting to realize just how much comic books had influenced our country's culture. Superheroic icons like Superman, Batman, Wonder Woman, Spider-Man and the Hulk had already made the leap to television and film; audiences knew who these characters were even if they had never read a comic book before.

The notion of comics as literature took greater hold through the maxi-series *Watchmen*, Frank Miller's gritty reinterpretation of Batman in *Batman: The Dark Knight Returns* (1986)–both taking a look at the superhero genre with more mature eyes while giving birth to the "grim 'n' gritty" label–and the Pulitzer Prize-winning two-part graphic novel *Maus* by Art Spiegelman that told a tale of the Holocaust with mice and cats standing in for human characters.

Another indication that comics and their readers were growing up was the release of DC's 12-issue *Crisis on Infinite Earths* (1985-86), an epic tale designed to clean house after decades of continuity had built up in the publisher's extensive superhero universe. Wiping the slate clean and reintroducing classic heroes like Superman and Batman with new origin stories, DC was acknowledging that the superhero genre was aging and took steps to reinvigorate its characters. Marvel also teamed up its entire superhero pantheon in the 1984 12-issue epic, *Marvel Super-Heroes: The Secret Wars*, which introduced a new black costume for Spider-Man.

While the heroes dealt with their cosmic crises, a variety of independent publishers continued to offer their own blend of superheroics and genre-busting stories, sometimes in stark black and white. Dark Horse, First, Eclipse, Comico, and Mirage gave us titles like *Fish Police*, *Grendel*, *Grimjack*, *E-Man*, *Nexus*, *Rocketeer*, *Miracleman*, and *Jon Sable, Freelance*.

ADVENTURES OF SUPERMAN #424
1987. DC Comics.

AMAZING SPIDER-MAN #252
1984. Marvel Comics.

AMAZING SPIDER-MAN ANNUAL #21
1987. Marvel Comics.

BATMAN #428
1988. DC Comics. Death of Robin (Jason Todd).

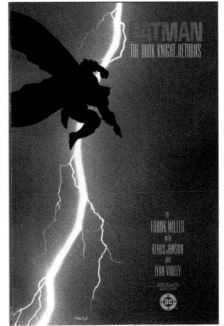

BATMAN: THE DARK KNIGHT RETURNS #1
1986. DC Comics.

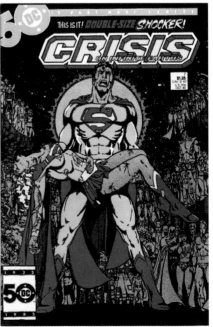

CRISIS ON INFINITE EARTHS #7
1985. DC Comics.

1984 - 1992

GHOST RIDER #15
1991. Marvel Comics.

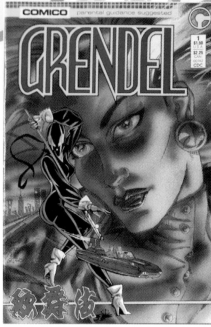

GRENDEL #1
1986. Comico.

THE MAN OF STEEL #1
1986. DC Comics.

SANDMAN & DEATH

Morpheus, Lord of the Dreaming, was the protagonist of Neil Gaiman's sophisticated and artistically innovative comic book series, *The Sandman*. One of seven siblings known as "The Endless," Morpheus has also been called The Prince of Stories, The Sandman, or simply Dream. With his siblings Destiny, Death, Destruction, Desire, Despair and Delirium, Dream has existed since the dawn of time and he has touched the lives of countless people.

Dream is initially introduced as haughty and cruel after years of imprisonment. Readers soon learned that the challenge of changing old ways is an enormous one for a

MARVEL SUPER-HEROES SECRET WARS #1
1984. Marvel Comics.

THE 'NAM #1
1986. Marvel Comics.

THE PUNISHER #1
1986. Marvel Comics.

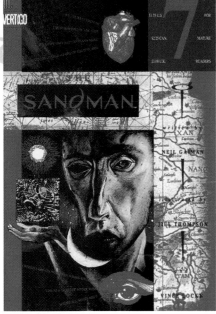

SANDMAN #47
1993. Vertigo/DC Comics.

SOLAR, MAN OF THE ATOM #1
1991. Valiant Comiics.

SPIDER-MAN #1
1990. Marvel Comics.

being who has had a routine for billions of years.

The series ran for 75 issues from 1988-1996 and was the flagship title in DC's Vertigo imprint, quickly becoming one of the most widely respected comics of its time; it even won the World Fantasy Award for Best Short Fiction in 1991 for #19's "A Midsummer Night's Dream."

The Sandman demonstrated that comic books could be high-quality literature and art, garnering respect for the craft of writing comics and helping to shape the genre of "sophisticated suspense" which focuses on elements of horror, fantasy and surrealism. The series also proved that a non-superhero comic book could still be successful.

TEENAGE MUTANT NINJA TURTLES #1
1984. Mirage Studios.

WATCHMEN #1
1986. DC Comics.

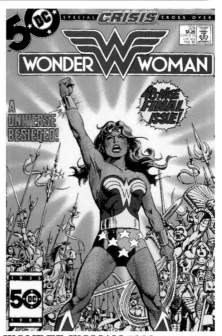

WONDER WOMAN #329
1986. DC Comics.

Image Comics was formed in 1992 by a team of artists who decided to leave Marvel and strike out on their own. Their brand of edgy, often violent and controversial superheroics, anchored by titles like *Spawn* and *Youngblood*, marked the end of the Copper Age and the beginning of a new approach, not only to comic book storytelling but its marketing as well.

An explosion of gimmick covers featuring holograms or foil and a bewildering array of variant editions hit the stands in the '90s as publishers targeted dedicated comic book collectors. As with many such trends, this one soon overstayed its welcome.

The pop culture centerpiece of this era was "The Death of Superman," an event covered by everyone from TV network news to *Time* and *Newsweek*. Battling the monster Doomsday, Superman appeared to meet his final end only to be replaced by a team of would-be Supermen in a multi-issue storyline that naturally culminated in the resurrection of the one true Superman. Phenomenal sales of the January 1993 death issue, *Superman* Vol. 2 #75 (sold in black plastic), once again focused mainstream media attention on superheroes and comics. And in 1996, just under 60 years after their first 'date,' Lois Lane and Superman were finally married.

Marvel reimagined its heroes several times, recruiting Image creators for the "Heroes Reborn" series and introducing an *Ultimate* imprint that relaunched their key characters with a fresh approach for a new, younger audience.

Regularly published Disney comics returned via Gemstone Publishing, Terry Moore offered comic book readers a long-running saga of romance and intrigue with *Strangers in Paradise*, and universe-altering storylines from DC and Marvel once again reshaped the superhero landscape. The heroes remain at the forefront as comics continue to explore their full potential as a literary art form in the 21st century.

9-11 VOLUME 2
2002. DC Comics.

AMAZING SPIDER-MAN #375
1993. Marvel Comics.

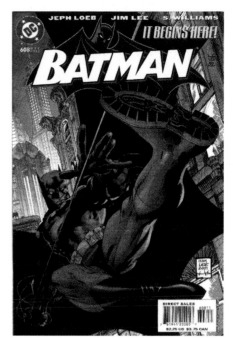

BATMAN #608
2002. DC Comics.

BLOODSHOT #0
1993. Valiant Comics.

BUFFY THE VAMPIRE SLAYER #1
1998. Dark Horse Comics.

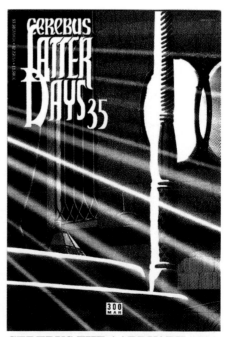

CEREBUS THE AARDVARK #300
2004. Aardvark-Vanaheim.

269

GROO THE WANDERER #120
1995. Marvel Comics.

HEROES
2001. Marvel Comics.

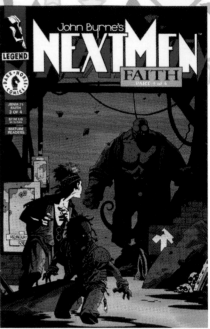

JOHN BYRNE'S NEXT MEN #21
1993. Dark Horse Comics.

SPAWN (IN PLASTIC)

In 1994, superstar artist and Image Comics co-founder, Todd McFarlane, set out to produce the most detailed and artistically accurate action figures on the market.

Based on *Spawn*, the character with which he launched Image Comics and started a mini-revolution in superhero storytelling, McFarlane contracted with some of the best sculptors in the world to create a line of action figures that more closely resembled statues than toys and brought comics to life. Since that time, more than twenty-two lines of *Spawn* figures have been produced, selling millions of figures worldwide.

In 1996, McFarlane Toys

MARVELS #1
1994. Marvel Comics.

MICKEY SPILLANE'S MIKE DANGER #1
1995. Tekno Comix.

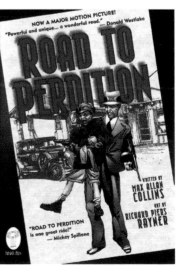

ROAD TO PERDITION
1998. DC Comics/Paradox Press.

SPAWN #1
1992. Image Comics.

SUPERMAN VOL. 2 #75
1993. DC Comics.

UNCANNY X-MEN #300
1993. Marvel Comics.

launched a Collector's Club which offered fans the chance to get exclusive action figures in members-only sales. Today the club has more than 100,000 members worldwide.

While the *Spawn* license is still the cornerstone of the company, McFarlane Toys has expanded to include film licenses for such films as *Austin Powers, Shrek, The Matrix, Terminator 3* and *Army of Darkness,* all four major North American sports, video games and even figures based on musical groups and the US military. When McFarlane and his fellow creators established Image Comics, little did anyone know that soon McFarlane Toys would raise the bar for comic- and media-based toys for years to come.

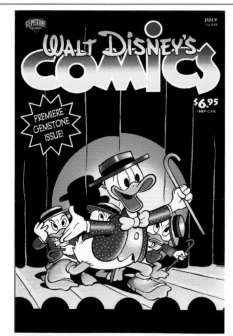

WALT DISNEY'S COMICS AND STORIES #634
2003. Gemstone Publishing.

WALT DISNEY'S UNCLE SCROOGE #319
2003. Gemstone Publishing.

YOUNGBLOOD #1
1992. Image Comics.

The Diamond Comic Distributors
Family of Companies

Diamond Comic Distributors
www.diamondcomics.com

Diamond International Galleries
www.diamondgalleries.com

Morphy Auctions
www.morphyauctions.com

Hake's Americana & Collectibles
www.hakes.com

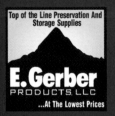

Geppi's Memorabilia Road Show
www.gmrs.com

Diamond Book Distributors
www.diamondbookdistributors.com

E. Gerber Products
www.egerber.com

Alliance Game Distributors
www.alliance-games.com

Diamond Select Toys & Collectibles
www.diamondselecttoys.com

Baltimore Magazine
www.baltimoremag.com

Gemstone Publishing
www.gemstonepub.com